For Iszi

1.
To Town Centre
To Inner Nobridge
2.
3
5.
6.
7.
4.
Tuesday Way
Crescent Lane Road
8.
9.
10.
11.
12
Mild Disappointment Way
13.
To Middling Otherbridge

14.

15.

Outer
Eastbridge

Lower
Upperbridge

Inner
Nobridge

Middling
Otherbridge

Upper
Lowerbridge

N
W E
S

1. Doodad's Shop
2. Dry Cleaner
3. Snorkel Supply Shop
4. Harp Shop
5. The Appledumps
6. Aunt Tabitha
7. Mr. Borris
8. Greta Zargo

9. Brigadier Ryefoot-fforwerd
10. Jessica Plumb
11. Mr and Mrs Jamali
12. Mr Teachbaddly
13. Wet Cleaner
14. The Cohens
15. The Merridews
16. Mrs Hummock

To the
Toothpaste Mines →

Upper
Lowerbridge
&
Environs

16.

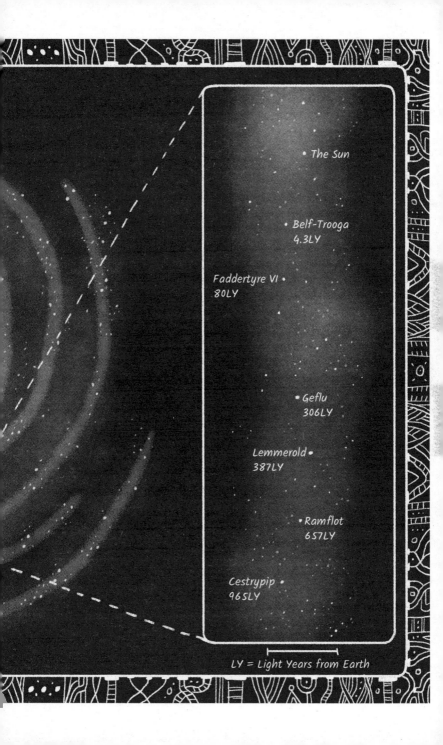

PROLOGUE

Earth

LAST SUNDAY

NO ONE ON Earth knew that their planet was being observed.

No one realised that vast computer brains waited, hidden in high Earth orbit, plotting and planning the planet's destruction.

No one detected the silvery robot as it descended from the blue summer's sky with a slow, quiet whoosh of unknown energy and flew towards the small English town of Middling Otherbridge.

No one knew that only three things stood in the way of their complete and utter annihilation: one elderly parrot, one eleven-year-old spelling mistake and one intrepid young newspaper-reporter-cum-schoolgirl in search of a Big Scoop.

And yet, that's exactly what's at stake in this book: *the fate of the entire planet Earth*.

Now read on ...

CHAPTER ONE

Upper Lowerbridge, England, Earth

LAST MONDAY

WHEN GRETA ZARGO'S parents accidentally died she was left the family home, everything in it, a large bank account, a library card, three hamsters (now dead, stuffed and on the mantelpiece), a lifetime subscription to *Clipboarding Weekly* magazine (*the* magazine for all clipboarding enthusiasts) and a pair of scissors she was to never run with. Since she had only been a baby at the time, all of this was held in trust for her by her Aunt Tabitha until her eighth birthday.*

As soon as she turned eight Greta moved out of her aunt's house and into her own one, just over the road. Naturally her aunt kept an eye on Greta, whenever she remembered to, and in the three years that followed absolutely no disasters had occurred. Other than perhaps that one time the fire engine had to come to get her off the roof. But even then, as Greta pointed out in a stiffly worded letter to the school newspaper, she hadn't *actually* been stuck. So, no disasters at all.

It was in the bathroom of that very house that Greta Zargo was now hiding underneath the bubbles in a deep, hot bath she'd

* The relevant sentence in her parents' Last Will and Testament should, of course, have read 'eighteenth birthday' but contained a legally binding spelling mistake. (It should be noted that this is not the spelling mistake mentioned in the Prologue; that's a different one made around the same time.)

6

run for herself. She soaked in the steaming tub, and breathed deep of the foamy perfume. This wasn't the best idea since it tickled her nose and made her sneeze, which blew a hole in the bubbles through which she could see the bathroom ceiling.

The ceiling, being a little grey at the edges, reminded her of her disappointing morning.

It was the summer and, being a girl of sparky determination, she'd got herself a holiday job as a Very Junior Reporter for *The Local Newspaper*.* It wasn't a real holiday job, since there are laws against employing eleven-year-old children, but when she'd followed Mr Inglebath (the newspaper's editor) across the park, through the library and into the swimming pool, asking to work for him, she had seemed so like a girl who

* *The Local Newspaper was an award-winning newspaper, as it proudly boasted on the front cover. It had won the Most Accurately Titled Print Periodical Prize four years running, until the Adverts for Old Fridges (incorporating Gossip & Photos of Local People) Weekly beat it to the top spot last time round.*

7

wouldn't take no for an answer that he'd said yes.

He quickly explained, however, that he wasn't going to pay her (though she was welcome to a biscuit or two whenever she visited the office).

This was fine by Greta. She wasn't in it for the money.

She had bought herself a new reporter's notebook and her aunt had made her a press badge with a tiny tape recorder hidden inside it.

When you pressed the button labelled 'Press' on the press badge it recorded everything it heard, which meant she didn't need to use the reporter's notebook to take notes, unless the press badge had run out of batteries, which it sometimes did. So, with the press badge pinned to her jacket and the notebook in her bag, just in case, she was ready to go out and report the news.

Oh, she had been so excited, and then ...

The problem was that as a Very Junior Reporter it was her job to go where her editor sent her and to cover the stories he told her to cover. That was just the way of things, and this morning Mr Inglebath had sent her to talk to Hari Socket about his missing Battenberg cake (he'd bought it for his son's birthday and had taken it out of the wrapper and put it on a plate in the kitchen from where it had mysteriously vanished while he was watching *Stop! Look! Redecorate!* in the front room). It had taken Greta two minutes and twenty-three seconds of investigation for her to realise this was *a rubbish story*. This was not *front page material*, and never would be, not unless a whole lot more cakes went missing, and what was the likelihood of that happening?

Had Greta been asked to explain exactly why she needed a bigger story to make her happy, she could have pointed to three very important reasons.

Firstly, halfway through the summer term she'd been kicked off the school newspaper for having published those photographs of the Head kissing Mr Biggingstock in the stationery cupboard. Being told that she couldn't be a reporter any more made Greta more determined than ever to be a reporter (in the same way that, when as a very young girl Aunt Tabitha had once told her not to eat soap, she proceeded to demolish two whole bars before burping bubbles for the rest of the week). When school started up again in September, she'd write in her 'What I did during the holidays' story: *I became an Ace Reporter and got the Big Scoop.*

would win her the Prilchard-Spritzer Medal, the quite famous award for great journalism.

It was a beautiful medal and would look lovely displayed above the mantelpiece next to her swimming certificate and the Best in Show rosette her mother had won once with a particularly handsome terrapin. Just think how *that* would look when she got back to school: *Sacked School Reporter Scoops Sensational Reporter Prize.* That would show them doubly. Twice over. Extra! Extra! Read all about it!

Lying back in the bath with great mountains of foam drifting around her, Greta shut her eyes, dozed and dreamt of the day Mr Prilchard* himself would loop the medal's ribbon around her neck. The wavering floral scent of the bubble bath hid the smell of fish that always followed Mr Prilchard around (even an imaginary Mr Prilchard in

* *Mr Prilchard owned Prilchard's Pilchards (and other Fish), the fishmonger's who sponsored the prize.*

14

a daydream) and Greta smiled broadly.

As she began her acceptance speech a bell rang.

That's odd, she thought.

As she began her short list of *thank you*s and longer list of *I told you so*s again, the bell rang a second time.

She woke up in the bath realising that it was actually the doorbell ringing.

Grabbing a towel, she stepped on to the toilet, pushed open the fanlight at the top of the bathroom window and peered out.

There was no one there.

'That's odd,' she said to herself.

She had heard, just before she reached the window, a slow quiet whoosh of unknown energy and, assuming it was the asthmatic blackbird* that liked to hang out in the big oak tree across the road, she ignored it.

* *The slow quiet whoosh of unknown energy had actually been a silvery robot floating above her doorstep, which flew off as she opened the window.*

15

Getting back in the bath, she found her daydream rather spoilt. The assembled crowd had mostly gone home and it seemed silly reading her acceptance speech to the few who remained, since they were mostly just there for the free buffet.

She got out of the bath and made herself some toast instead.

CHAPTER TWO

Cestrypip

965 LIGHT YEARS FROM EARTH
107,242 YEARS AGO

THE PEOPLE OF the planet Cestrypip had a unique life cycle: like insects on Earth they went through a series of stages.

After a five year period as a large, wriggling white grub, and a further fifty or sixty years as a green-skinned, lizardish humanoid doing all the usual stuff humanoids do (having jobs, arguing about sports

17

and giving birth to large, white maggoty grubs) the Cestrypippians would give away all their possessions, say farewell to their families and put down roots, put out leaves and spend a century as a slow-dreaming tree. When the dream was ended, they would shed their bark, pull their feet from the soil and spend a vigorous decade in their final life stage as a shouty but encouraging PE teacher.

It was during his humanoid life stage that the great Cestrypian scientist Harknow-Bumfurly-Histlock formed a plan to explore and investigate the entire galaxy.

He talked the people of his world into taking apart some of the other, less import-ant planets in their solar system and using them to build a fleet of Huge Space-Going Robots (each filled with a host of smaller robots) which they would send flying out to nearby star systems to explore and investigate and compile detailed reports on.

Within a few centuries of their launch, the first giant space-going robots started beaming back images of new planets, strange stars and amusingly shaped asteroids for the Cestrypippians to compile into the fabled *Harknow-Bumfurly-Histlock Big Book of Galactic*

Facts™, the ultimate collection of galactic information, stored in enormous computers buried deep beneath the Croomock mountain range and powered by the magma heart of the planet itself.

And so it began.

CHAPTER THREE

Upper Lowerbridge, England, Earth

LAST TUESDAY

'SO, MRS HUMMOCK,' Greta Zargo said (as she pressed 'Press' on her press badge). 'Give me the facts. Just the facts.'

'Pardon?'

(Mrs Hummock, a lady of early late middle age with large blonde hair, a small grey beard and extravagant purple-rimmed glasses, had opened the door to find a little girl standing there smiling at her. The little girl had said she was writing a story for *The Local Newspaper*, which had sounded quite sweet, but now that the questioning had begun Mrs Hummock was beginning to have doubts.)

'What sort of cake was it?'

'It was a sponge,' Mrs Hummock said, 'with peanut butter fondant icing. You see, Mrs Wedlock likes –'

'This cake,' Greta interrupted, not wanting to hear about Mrs Wedlock.* It was important to keep the focus on the facts. 'Where was it when it went missing?'

Greta had her notepad out and tapped it urgently with her short pencil.

'When it went missing?' Mrs Hummock asked.

'That's what I said. Quit stalling, lady.'

Greta had read more than the usual amount of detective novels for a girl her age. Her mother had been a fan of Augusta Crispy and had left a complete set of her novels on the third shelf down in the second bedroom. This was *exactly* how the private eyes in them spoke.

Mrs Hummock looked puzzled for a moment, huffed, and then said, 'But if I *knew* where it was when it went missing, it wouldn't be missing, would it?'

* Mrs Wedlock was Mrs Hummock's gossip partner. The two of them got together several times a week to share rumours and say rude things about everyone else in the town. Mrs Hummock did the talking while Mrs Wedlock did the tutting, but Greta already knew that.

23

Greta sighed. This being-an-investigative-reporter business was hard work when you went face to face with the intellectual giants of Upper Lowerbridge.

'Mrs Hummock,' she said, looking sternly at the woman through narrowed eyes, 'why are you being so unhelpful? What is it you've got to hide? Did your cake *really* go missing, or did you just eat it? Is that it? Mrs Wedlock comes round for afternoon tea and you're too embarrassed to admit you've already eaten the cake? You make up some ridiculous story about a cake theft to cover your embarrassment? But then the police are called and they dust your kitchen for fingerprints and now there's no way you can get back to the truth. Not without being arrested for wasting police time. Is that it? Did *you* eat the cake, Mrs Hummock? Did you *eat* it?'

Mrs Hummock stood slightly dazed and windswept by the unexpected force of Greta's questions, her mouth hanging slack and her glasses askew. Eleven-year-old girls were supposed to be nicer than this. They were supposed to respect their elders.

After a moment Mrs Hummock closed her mouth.

After another moment she spoke.

'I'm going to talk to Wilf about this,' she said, before slamming the front door in Greta's face.

Wilf was Wilfred Inglebath, Greta's boss, who was also Mrs Hummock's brother-in-law.

Greta walked up the path with a slump in her shoulders.

It had turned out that Hari Socket's Battenberg *had* just been the beginning of things. When Sophie Doodad (in the corner shop) had told her that Mrs Hummock's cake had gone missing too, she'd rushed round, eager to get an exclusive.

But she'd been *too* eager. She'd let the little whiff of a Big Scoop make her forget who she was. Forgot *where* she was. She'd started acting like a hard-nosed detective from the big city rather than a small-time summer-holiday schoolgirl-cum-journalist from the not-exactly-bustling small country town.

Five minutes later she cycled into her street and up on to the pavement outside her house.

'Hi, Greta,' said Jessica Plumb, the girl from number five who was Greta's best friend and let her copy her answers in maths lessons.

'There was a big silvery robot asking after you earlier. It said it would call again. Flew off with a slow, quiet whoosh. A bit like that blackbird. The asthmatic one.'

Greta had too much on her mind right then to pay attention to what Jessica was saying, so she smiled, nodded and went 'Uh-huh' as she dropped her bike on the grass of the front garden.

'I'm excited about the Cohens' party on Friday,' Jessica said, bouncing a little. 'I'm starting work on my costume tonight, but I'm not going to tell you what it is. I want it to be a surprise. Mum's bought me some extra tin foil though.'

'Tin foil,' said Greta, for the sake of saying something.

(Jessica was so good at her side of a conversation that Greta never needed to say very much to keep her happy, which was fortunate because Greta never really knew what to say to Jessica. It wasn't that she didn't like her – Jessica *was* her best friend. It was more that Greta was never quite sure what friends were actually for … what you were supposed to *do* with them.)

'Cheerio,' Greta said as she opened her front door.

'Cheerio,' waved Jessica from the pavement.

Greta went indoors, and as she was wondering how she could write up her very short interview, the telephone rang.

'Hello?'

'Greta?'

'Yes, Mr Inglebath?'

'I want a word with you, young lady.'

'Yes, Mr Inglebath?'

'Do you know what that word is?'

'No, Mr Inglebath.'

'*Fired*.'

'Oh, Mr Inglebath.'

She put the phone down.

She had a word for Mr Inglebath too, but being only eleven years old, and knowing her mother wouldn't have approved of her using *language**, refused to think it.

CHAPTER FOUR

Ramflot

657 LIGHT YEARS FROM EARTH
73,102 YEARS AGO

THE PEOPLE OF the planet Ramflot had been surprised by the appearance of a silvery floating robot in their caves, partly because they didn't see many silvery floating robots any more, but mostly because it was Thursday.

The Ramflottians never visited one another's caves on a Thursday. It had always been considered unlucky ever since Rarf had hit her head on an unexpected stalactite while visiting Glarf's cave on a Thursday three weeks before.

The inhabitants of this particular cave stared at the robot with wide eyes and narrow mouths.

'*Art flarge grongko pop pip*,' the hovering robot said, meaning, 'Take me to your leader.'

The robot had learnt the Ramflottian language from television signals it had picked up in space on its approach to the Ramflottian solar system. Unfortunately, in the time between the robot's learning the language and its arrival on Ramflot, a series of rather serious global wars had taken place, which explained why the last seventeen Ramflottians were all living in caves.*

Before the war there had been two languages spoken on Ramflot. Uniquely, both languages had consisted of exactly the same words, but each language used those words to mean different things. The upshot was, if you didn't check carefully which language the Ramflottian you were speaking to spoke, it was remarkably easy

* An intelligent species only lives in caves twice in its history, once on the way up and once on the way down.

spoken in the cave: 'Those yellow fruits, a bit like hinkleberries, *do* smell a lot like sadness, don't they?'

But meaning, in the Ramflottian language off the television: 'Here. This is our leader, just here.'

The floating robot, turning to Harrerf: *'Crumk bilf tiffle pop pip pop?'*

Meaning, in the Ramflottian language off the television: 'Please may we have your planet?'

But meaning, in the Ramflottian language spoken in the cave: 'How tall is your aunt, not including her hat?'

Harrerf, shrugging: *'Grampf.'*

Meaning, in the Ramflottian language spoken in the cave: 'Huh? I do not have an aunt, and she does not have a hat. Who are you, strange intruder-into-Thursday?

Maybe you should come back tomorrow, and ask about my uncle.'

But meaning, unfortunately, in the Ramflottian language off the television: 'Yes, take our planet.'

The silvery robot said thank you (or *'Plike afgoff rilp felp dagog burf werf wilf pip pap aggle cade cathell brime welf paddlog'*, which was about the only phrase that was the same in both Ramflottian languages*) and drifted away with a slow, quiet whoosh of unknown energy into the Ramflottian sky.

These sorts of coincidental conversations are *exactly* what keep the universe running the way it does, which is proof, some philosophers suggest, if any were needed, that there must be a much better organised universe somewhere else that we've not been invited to.

* *That and 'Pilf foolp flartle dawg' of course, which meant 'My silver jumpsuit has been at the dry cleaner's since Monday'.*

36

*   *   *

Once the silvery robot had reported the answer back to the Huge Space-Going Robot, a thousand other small silvery robots of different shapes and sizes emerged from its insides and flew towards Ramflot.

The robots circled around, taking measurements and photographs and recording all the important stuff before they dismantled the planet.

All the rocks and metals and gases that had once been the planet Ramflot were used to build another six Huge Space-Going Robots, each filled with a thousand smaller silvery robots, and all aimed at other nearby star systems judged by their vast computer brains as being ripe and ready for exploration.

And, finally, the original Huge Space-Going Robot transformed itself into an enormous round blue space station orbiting Ramflot's sun, just as Ramflot once had. It turned its antennae toward that little spot of space where the home planet Cestrypip was and beamed back all the information it had collected about Ramflot and its seventeen inhabitants.

Off into space flew images of them and of the Ramflottian flora and fauna, along with details of its size and position and how many moons it had had, and copies of the television programmes it had recorded on its long approach to the planet: information that would become a brand new in-depth entry in the *Harknow-Bumfurly-Histlock Big Book of Galactic Facts*™.

CHAPTER FIVE

Upper Lowerbridge, England, Earth

LAST WEDNESDAY

SOPHIE DOODAD RAN the shop on the corner.

Greta had popped in to buy some sherbet and a pair of rubber gloves.

'There's been another 'nother theft,' Sophie had whispered as she handed Greta her change.

'Another 'nother theft?' Greta had asked.

'Another 'nother cake's gone missing,' Sophie had whispered, tapping the side of her nose.

'Oh,' Greta had replied.

'Swiss roll,' Sophie had whispered, looking around to make sure they weren't being listened to. 'Oscar Teachbaddly.'

Greta's brain had buzzed.

'Thought you should know,' Sophie had whispered.

'Thanks,' Greta had said.

She hadn't had the heart to tell Sophie that she didn't need to know, not any more, not since she'd been fired from the newspaper.

But she was still thinking about Mr Teachbaddly's vanishing Swiss roll as she pottered about in the garden later that morning. (Not having any parents left to do the gardening meant that she did it herself. *⤵

* Aunt Tabitha attempted to help out now and then. For example, she'd once made Greta an automatic spade to help with the digging, but once it had been switched on they had been unable to switch it off, since Aunt Tabitha had misplaced the remote control. It had dug and dug and dug. So now, Greta simply didn't go near that end of the garden any more. Sometimes when she looked out of an upstairs window at night, she saw a flickering glow from deep in the hole reflecting up on to the undersides of the trees.

43

Over the years she'd grown a wide variety of weeds, tangles and both under- and overgrowth. There was, however, a small patch of carefully cultivated flower bed near the back door that she actually kept looking neat. And this was where she was pottering as she thought.)

There was nothing she wanted more than to rush round to Mr Teachbaddly's house and ask him some Very Nosy Questions.

'Was there anyone else in the house when the cake went missing? How long were you upstairs for? Were there any doors or windows open?' (It had been a warm evening, stuffy and sticky, she remembered.)

'Ouch!' she said suddenly, pulling her hand away with a sting of pain.

She'd not been concentrating on what she was doing and one of Aunt Tabitha's clawberries had bitten her. *

It had bitten quite deep and there was blood pooling on the back of her hand.

Giving the clawberry plant a stern stare, which was entirely pointless since the clawberry didn't have any eyes to see the stern stare with, Greta clambered to her feet and headed back to the kitchen to clean the bite and find a plaster.

As the water gushed out of the tap and the pipes gurgled and clanked (she really needed to get someone to come and look at those) the doorbell rang.

'Just a minute,' she shouted.

But by the time she'd dried her hand off and pressed the plaster in place, whoever had rung the bell had gone away.

* Aunt Tabitha had developed the clawberry, a strawberry plant that was trained in self-defence, as another attempt to make gardening easier. No slug survived an encounter with the clawberry, and the more slugs the clawberry ate, the fatter and juicier its berries became (which was nice, even if they tasted a little of slug).

She stood at the open door, smelling a faint whiff of something strange, looking at an empty patch of front path and not noticing the quietly whooshing silvery robot floating away above her head.

CHAPTER SIX

Lemmerold

387 LIGHT YEARS FROM EARTH
42,973 YEARS AGO

LEMMEROLD WAS INHABITED by highly talk-ative blimp-like beings who drifted through algae-like clouds. They siphoned food from the air with their many eating-holes, while simultaneously singing the songs of their people with their many singing-holes.

They sang very loudly, and their songs contained all the gossip, all the wisdom, all the boasts, all the histories and all the knowledge that the Lemmeroldians had gathered over the centuries of their drifting, airborne lives.

The reason they sang so loudly was that Lemmeroldians didn't get on very well with one another. (Mainly because of all the gossip, wisdom, boasts, histories and knowledge that other Lemmeroldians insisted on singing when they should have been listening to *my* song, they each thought.)

It had been lifetimes since any Lemmeroldian had actually heard what any other Lemmeroldian had to say, and so most of the gossip, wisdom, boasts, histories and knowledge was long out of date, fairly out of tune and totally unnecessary.

When the silvery robot landed on the back of one of the large, floating, drifting, singing Lemmeroldians, it spoke to a pik. (Piks were a small, intelligent, triangular-ish race with no ears, who farmed the barndub fields that grew on the mist-swathed backs of the Lemmeroldians.)

'Take me to your leader,' it said.

The pik said nothing, but looked at the robot as if it had never seen a large, silvery floating metal thing with flashing lights before. (Which it hadn't.)

The Lemmeroldian it was stood on had just finished a long verse about why greenish purple algae-like clouds are better than purple-ish green algae-like clouds, and was beginning a new verse about how someone called Quallllm had once borrowed a flowmp-droffer from someone called Qualllum and had not yet given it back.

As the pik felt the familiar, comforting rumble of the Lemmeroldian's song change and shift beneath its feet, it understood that everything was perfectly normal, even with this never-before-seen metal thing flashing lights at it. The pik knelt down and patted the good, comforting Lemmeroldian. Then it stood up, got on with hoeing the damp skin-soil and ignored the New Thing.

The robot interpreted the pik's patting as meaning 'Here is my leader,' which wasn't entirely incorrect.

It floated down to hover beside the giant eyeball of the singing, drifting Lemmeroldian and, having studied the creature's song for several hours, sang, 'Please may we have your planet?' quite loudly and slightly out of tune.

'*"Yes, yes, yes, of course! A hundred times yes," said Quallllm,*' sang the Lemmeroldian, ignoring the robot, just as it had ignored the rest of its singing species for thousands of years. It continued its operatic warble:

Again Quallllm said, 'Yes.'
Flowmp-droffer was useless at that time
of year,

but had he known ... had he known!
A quarter solar cycle later he would need it.
Need it a lot!
But where was Qualllum now?
Where was Qualllum?
And where, oh, where was the flowmp-droffer?

... and so on, for several weeks.

But the silvery robot had listened no further than the first 'yes' before it flew off with a slow, quiet whoosh of unknown energy.

                            *   *   *

The Lemmeroldians continued singing the
songs of their people, and the piks continued tending to their barndub fields, right up
until the planet no longer existed.

   Images of the planet and its inhabitants,
measurements and recordings, beamed
across the depths of darkest space towards
the planet Cestrypip to become another
entry in the *Harknow-Bumfurly-Histlock Big
Book of Galactic Facts*™.

CHAPTER SEVEN

Upper Lowerbridge, England, Earth

LAST THURSDAY, BREAKFAST-TIME

WHEN GRETA TRIED to have her breakfast she discovered that the cornflake packet contained two cornflakes. It wasn't much of a breakfast for a young lady of her height and haircut.

She gave a deep sigh but tipped them into a bowl nevertheless.

When she went to the fridge to get

some milk to put on top of them, she discovered she had plenty of milk. A big bottle, nearly full.

As she tipped it, however, the bottle slipped and a great big glug of milk sloshed out, filling the bowl and splashing all over the countertop.

The two cornflakes were swept away, over the edge of the counter, along the kitchen floor and under the washing machine.

Greta put the milk bottle down and stared at the mess.

Even though two cornflakes weren't much, she'd still been looking forward to them.

She had tried to make toast for her supper last night, but the bread had gone mouldy.

The biscuit barrel looked like it had

biscuits in, but they were just the paintings of biscuits on the side of the jar.

There was sherbet in the cupboard, but she was saving that for her lunch.

It was at times like this that she almost wished her mum and dad hadn't died in that marshmallow factory accident. One of them would've gone up to Doodad's corner shop and bought some more corn-flakes for her. Greta was in her pyjamas and she didn't fancy going out like that and she didn't have anyone else to send, so she just sat at the kitchen table and drank milk from the bowl with a spoon.

And then, suddenly, unexpectedly, there was a knock at the doorbell.

She half-smiled and half-sighed.

The only person she knew who knocked on her doorbell (three short, sharp rings) was Aunt Tabitha, and Greta didn't know if she could face her today. She was always so jolly and Greta didn't feel jolly in the slightest. She felt like a failure. No parents. No breakfast. No job.

No Big Scoop.

Slump.

The letterbox rattled.

'Rise and shine. Cooee! Greta. Up and at 'em. Cooee!' her aunt called through the oblong slot.

'I'm not in,' shouted Greta. 'I'm still in bed. I've gone to the shops. I'm on Mars.'

A key rattled in the lock and the front door opened.

'Morning, darling,' Aunt Tabitha said, looking her up and down and plonking some bubbling cheese on toast on the table. 'I heard what happened from Wilf.'*

* Wilf Inglebath was Aunt Tabitha's second cousin by marriage. Upper Lowerbridge was one of those towns where most of the people were related in one way or another.

'Oh yes?' said Greta.

'I must say,' her aunt went on as she poured some hot chocolate from a flask into a cup, 'I gave him a piece of my mind.'

'Which piece?'

'Number 8.'

That was, Greta knew from experience, quite a serious piece.

PIECE 8.

She mumbled some extra thanks as she gobbled the cheese on toast.

'I don't think I'll be getting a Christmas card from him this year,' Tabitha said.

'I didn't mean to get you in trouble, Auntie,' said Greta as she sipped the hot chocolate.

'Don't be so silly, Greta,' her aunt said, opening the fridge and looking inside. 'You know I don't care about Christmas cards, and anyway I expect by Christmas he'll have forgotten he's not sending me one and it'll probably turn up just as normal.'

Greta poked at her half-empty bowl of milk with her spoon. She had a feeling bubbling deep in her stomach that was saying two things to her. Firstly it was saying, *Greta, when you get back to school you won't have anything interesting to write in your 'What I did during the summer holidays' essay, and the Head will have won.* And secondly it said, *Greta, cakes have been going missing left, right and centre and only you can find out why.*

'Auntie,' she said, not listening to her stomach. 'I'm going back to bed. I'm going to stay there until I'm old enough to not have to go back to school.'

'Oh,' said her aunt. 'If only I'd got the regenerating edible pyjamas to work, then maybe you could, but ... Or perhaps I could try a pillow-cake. Lavender-scented, maybe, to encourage sleep ...?'

'Cakes,' Greta mumbled. She explained to Aunt Tabitha about all the cakes that had gone missing in the last few days, and how she couldn't investigate the mystery now Mr Inglebath had sacked her.

'Pish and nonsense,' replied her aunt, banging the table. 'The Greta I know has been an investigative reporter from the day she solved the Riddle of the Missing Asparagus *

* *It had 'fallen' into Aunt Tabitha's handbag.*

62

when she was just four years old.'

'You still don't like asparagus, do you?' said Greta.

'No, and people still insist on serving it. I've had to build a bigger handbag.'

Greta smiled, and then stopped smiling.

'But Mr Inglebath fired me, Aunt,' she repeated.

'Did that stop you from solving the Mystery of the Unexpected Dalmatian?* You didn't have a job then, did you? In actual fact, you had a spelling test.'

'Which I failed.'

'Failing a spelling test is hardly the end of the world, darling. It's really not that important.'

Greta shrugged.

'Greta, dear,' her aunt went on, 'it's always *you* who has the presence of mind

* The school exchange party had arrived a week early, due to a funny misunderstanding.

and determination to look into these things, who cares enough about *The Truth* to hunt it down wherever it may be. Remember when you solved the Enigma of the Cross Bees?* Hmm?'

'OK, Auntie,' Greta said, standing up and filled with fire. 'Enough now! You're right. I can't just let this go. Cakes have gone missing and someone has to work out why and where and who and when and how and why and where. I was Mr Inglebath's best reporter –'

'Also his *only* reporter,' her aunt added. 'He's a fool to let you go.'

'– yes, and I bet *he's* not left the office to interview the victims himself. He'll have been too busy trying to do the crossword. There's still time. If I can solve the mystery and publish it myself –'

* They were cross because someone kept moving all the flowers a little bit to the right when they were asleep.

'You could use the photocopier in the library.'

'– then I'll still get the Big Scoop, and maybe even the Prilchard-Spritzer Medal.'

There was a new glint in her eyes, a new determination in her voice, a new plan in her head.

'I'm going to go and pay Mr Teachbaddly a visit.'

'Oh, darling,' said Aunt Tabitha, clapping her hands together. 'I'm so proud of you. Bravo, old sport! You are truly a Great Zargo, Greta Zargo!'

Greta went upstairs to have a shower and get dressed.

An investigative reporter will never be taken seriously if they are asking questions in their pyjamas. That was probably rule number one of being an investigative reporter, Greta reckoned. (If ever she were to write a book with tips on being an investigative reporter, that would definitely be in there.)

While Greta was upstairs the doorbell rang.

Aunt Tabitha was crunching toast when she answered it.

On the doorstep was a large silvery robot with flashing lights and robotic arm-like protrusions.

'Are you The Great Zargo?' it said, although because of the toast-crunching noise in her ears, Aunt Tabitha only heard the final word.

'Me? No,' said Aunt Tabitha, who was a scientist and therefore unflummoxed by robots and flashing lights. 'She's having a shower. Perhaps I can take a message for her?'

'Please may we have your planet?'

'I'm sorry?'

Something was happening on the pavement behind the robot, which had distracted Aunt Tabitha — a pigeon was arguing with a squirrel over an empty crisp packet that was fluttering down the street (possibly cheese and onion flavour).

'The message is: Please may we have your planet?' the robot said.

'Have your planet?' Aunt Tabitha repeated, not really listening but staring at the squirrel, which now had the pigeon in a neck-lock and was rubbing the top of the bird's head with its little squirrely knuckles. 'I'll be sure to pass it on. Will you call again later, perhaps?'

'Very well. We shall call again tomorrow, when The Great Zargo is available.'

'Excellent, excellent,' said Aunt Tabitha, as the silvery robot drifted up into the air with a slow, quiet whoosh of unknown energy.

When the smoke cleared the pigeon was sat, slightly stunned, on the pavement and the squirrel was nowhere to be seen. It had been a normal-sized squirrel, Aunt Tabitha noted, with a touch of disappointment.

Twenty minutes later, when Greta was washed and changed and ready to go out and ask Oscar Teachbaddly some hard questions, Aunt Tabitha stopped her in the hallway.

'I've just remembered the other reason I came round,' she said. 'It wasn't just toast and cheering up.' She'd already forgotten about the robot, which was often the way with Aunt Tabitha's mind. (It flitted about like a magpie in a washing machine.) 'I've managed to breed an amazing new experimental animal: a giant vegetarian squirrel. I thought it might be useful somehow, if only I can get rid of its peanut allergy. But when I went in on Monday the door to the giant vegetarian squirrel-house was open and the giant vegetarian squirrel wasn't anywhere in the garden. I looked on the bird table, behind the shed, along the top of the fence, under the settee. Nowhere. I thought he might come back when he got lonely, but he's not turned up yet. Just keep an eye out, would you, darling? He's called Jonathon. He's probably scared and lost and lonely.'

'Aren't squirrels already vegetarians?' Greta asked.

'That's the clever thing,' said Aunt Tabitha, not really by way of any sort of explanation.

They left the house and, at the end of the path, went different ways along the pavement, off into their different days, one to search for squirrels and one to track down a serial cake thief. *

* Not, it should be noted, a cereal cake thief. Not a single rice crispie cake or chocolate cornflake brownie went missing during the entire investigation.

CHAPTER EIGHT

Geflu

306 LIGHT YEARS FROM EARTH
34,111 YEARS AGO

THE GEFLUVIANS HAD already begun exploring their own solar system when the Huge Space-Going Cestrypian Robot arrived around their star.

They had moon bases and space stations and Gefluvians had even walked on Boflu, the fifth planet, and plans were afoot for a mission to Bagflu, the third planet.

When the silvery robot knocked at the door of Space Station B, Commander Wrigglesworth pressed the comm-link button and said, 'Hello? Can we help you?'

'Take me to your leader,' said the robot.

'That would be the President,' said the Commander, and gave it the President's address.

* * *

The President and her aides had a secret meeting with the robot. It went a bit like this:

The robot: 'Please may we have your planet?'

The President: 'What for?'

The robot: 'We need resources to continue our mission exploring the galaxy.'

The President: 'If we let you use our resources, what will we get in return?'

The robot: 'We can offer you information.'

The President: 'What sort of information?'

The robot: 'We can tell you about advanced mathematics and hyperspatial physics and star systems we have explored and aliens we have encountered and we have many pictures of amusingly shaped asteroids and –'

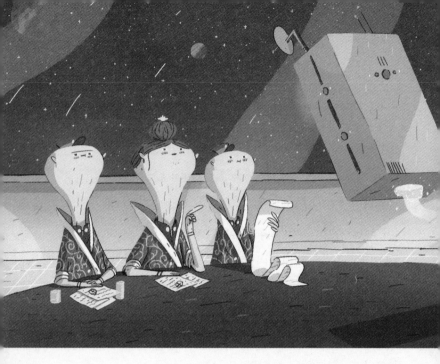

The President: 'Stop, stop, stop! You had me at "amusingly shaped asteroids".'

The robot: 'Then we can have your planet, please?'

The President: 'Play fair. *First* give us all that information, the pictures and stuff, *then* you can get what you need.'

The robot hovered in the air for a moment, lights blinking but saying nothing, and then it settled down again and said, 'The information has been transmitted into your computers. Now may we have your planet?'

The President was already chuckling at an asteroid shaped a bit like a welfpog and simply said, 'Yeah, sure, take what you need.'

Commander Wrigglesworth watched with a sinking feeling in his stomach from the window of Space Station B as a thousand silvery robots flew out of the Huge Space-Going Robot and carefully deconstructed his planet.

First the atmosphere was removed, then the crust was broken up and the glowing mantle extracted, and then the core was mined for iron.

The Huge Space-Going Robot used the raw materials to construct a dozen more

Huge Space-Going Robots, each one identical to itself.

Commander Wrigglesworth watched as these new Huge Space-Going Robots slowly accelerated out of the system, heading off to a dozen different stars, ones the original Huge Space-Going Robot hadn't explored yet.

'Oh,' he said, as he munched the very last packet of qualf-flakes in the universe. 'Oh dear.'

The Commander watched as the final Huge Space-Going Robot transformed itself into a round blue space station, half the size of the destroyed planet, covered with images and writing and emitting messages at all different wavelengths.

Through his telescope he saw pictures of Geflu (and of the people living on it) as it had been before the planet was destroyed. This was a Cestrypian Memory Station.

The Memory Station was filled with records of the vanished planet, and of the people who had been turned into raw materials along with the rocks and oceans. So, now, any space explorer who visits the Gefluvian star system will be able to learn about what was there before it wasn't there any more, and that the Cestrypippians got there first. (This was, of course, in addition to beaming all the information back to Cestrypip for inclusion in the *Harknow-Bumfurly-Histlock Big Book of Galactic Facts*™.)

'Well, I suppose that's all right then,' said Commander Wrigglesworth, scooting down a gravity-free corridor on Space Station B. He screwed up the empty qualf-flake packet and let it dangle in gravity-free mid-air behind him as he wondered what to do with the rest of his afternoon.

CHAPTER NINE

Upper Lowerbridge, England, Earth

LAST THURSDAY, LUNCHTIME

OSCAR TEACHBADDLY WAS rearranging his front garden when Greta approached. He kept it in six wheelbarrows for variety and ease of regular rearrangement. (When bored of how it looked, he would simply wheel one barrowful of plants, pond or shubbery into a different position and *hey presto!* the whole place looked like a new garden.)

'Mr Teachbaddly,' Greta said, tapping her notebook with a pen and pressing the button labelled 'Press' on her press badge. 'I'd like to ask you some questions.'

'Greta,' he said. 'How lovely to see you. Are you keeping well? You look well. Enjoying the holidays? Still dancing?'

Oscar Teachbaddly had taught Greta at

the Lower Upperbridge Infant School, which Greta had attended some years earlier.*⌒⟶ (He'd been very fond of English country dancing.)

'No,' she said. 'I'm not still dancing. Although I did very much enjoy it because of your lessons.' (This was called 'buttering up'. It's what a good and clever investigator did, Greta reckoned. She'd been *too* direct with Mrs Hummock, so now she was being more subtle. Say nice things, put Mr Teachbaddly at his ease … then she could pounce with the hard questions.)

'Oh, that's nice,' he said.

(That was probably enough buttering up, Greta thought.)

'I've come about the Swiss roll.'

'Swiss roll?'

'Yes, the Swiss roll.'

'What Swiss roll?'

'The missing Swiss roll.'

'Oh,' he said. 'That Swiss roll.'

'I need to ask you some questions.'

'The police have already been,' Oscar Teachbaddly said. 'They've already asked lots of questions.'

'Do I look like the police?' she said.

'No,' he answered.

(He was beginning to feel uncomfortable. Her voice was serious, her stare unwavering and the kipper he'd had for breakfast off.)

'Yours isn't the only cake to have gone missing. Did you know that?'

'I had heard something. Whispers.'

'Where was your cake when it vanished, Mr Teachbaddly?'

'It was on the arm of my armchair.'

'And where were you?'

'I was upstairs.'

'Was there anyone else in the house?'

'No, it was just me. Julian and Barry and Simon and Clive and Petros and Aaron and Sebastian and Esteban and Andrew and Big Derek and Sarah and Little Derek and Ivan were out at their quiz night. It was Wednesday, after all.'

'And when you came back downstairs?'

'They were still out.'

Greta thought she really ought to track down Julian and Barry and Simon and Clive and Petros and Aaron and Sebastian and Esteban and Andrew and Big Derek and Sarah and Little Derek and Ivan to confirm Mr Teachbaddly's story … or maybe, just this once, she could assume he was telling the truth.

'What about the cake, Mr Teachbaddly?'

'Oh. The cake? The cake was gone.'

'The plate?'

'On the floor.'

'Were there any crumbs, Mr Teachbaddly?'

'Crumbs?'

'Yes, crumbs.'

'Some.'

'Some crumbs?'

'Yes, some crumbs.'

Greta tapped her pen on her notepad as she thought. Maybe this was the big break she needed. She hadn't heard about crumbs being left behind at any of the other thefts. Maybe the thief was getting sloppy.

'Have you read the story of Hansel and Gretel, Mr Teachbaddly?'

'Maybe,' he said cautiously, unsure of where this conversation was going.

'So ... was there a trail, Mr Teachbaddly? Was there a trail of crumbs?'

He looked pale. He gulped.

'Yes,' he whispered.

She spoke quietly, so that he had to lean close to hear her.

'Where did they lead?'

'To the window,' he said, looking away.

'Was the window open?'

'Yes. But only a little. That's what's so strange.'

'Show me the window,' she said.

He pointed at the front room window, which was just behind them.

'It was that one,' he said.

It was a large window, made of a see-through material Greta reckoned was probably glass.* Along the top was a long, narrow rectangle of window that opened outwards. A fanlight. It was open a little right now.

'Was it like that?' she asked.

'Yes,' he said.

The gap was so small the cake thief must have been a tiny person: a little child maybe or someone who had come in contact with a shrink ray.*

She walked over to the wheelbarrow that was directly underneath the window. She pushed leaves and flowers aside and peered at the soft, deep, rich brown earth.

* Her aunt was the scientist; she would know.

* Her aunt was the scientist; she would know.

'What are you doing?' Oscar Teachbaddly asked.

'I'm investigating,' she said. 'You wouldn't understand. We're not dancing now, Mr Teachbaddly.'

She was looking for footprints. Someone lowering themselves from the window would have landed in that wheelbarrow and they would've left a footprint in the soft, deep, rich, brown earth, surely? But look as hard as she could, there didn't seem to be a footprint to be found.

Maybe it was a wild goose chase. Maybe the thief hadn't come out this way. Maybe the trail of crumbs was misleading, a red herring, a clue too good to be true. Maybe Oscar Teachbaddly had eaten the cake then had a brief touch of amnesia, or maybe the thief had gone out the back door (which had

been open, it being quite a balmy evening).
Oh! There were just too many possibilities
and yet she had felt so close.

She looked up at the long, narrow open
window.

There was a small red smear on the glass.

She climbed into the wheelbarrow (there
were definitely footprints in it now*), up
on to the window sill and peered closer.

There was a crumb stuck to the red
smear. It looked like a cake crumb.

She made a quick sketch on her notepad
and then touched the red smear with her
fingertip.

It was sticky.

It smelt like jam.

'What's this?' she said, spinning round and
holding her finger out to Mr Teachbaddly as if
she expected him to taste it.

And three broken geraniums.

'It looks like …'

'Jam,' she declared, licking it.

'That means …'

'Yes! The Swiss roll thief *definitely* escaped through your window, taking the cake with him or her. And then they *vanished*.'

* * *

Greta sat in her kitchen going over what she knew so far.

She listened back to the conversations with Hari Socket and Mrs Hummock and with Oscar Teachbaddly that her press badge had recorded when she'd pressed the button labelled 'Press', and wrote the important bits down.

She was beginning to see patterns here. If only she could put them all together to build  the big picture ... Soon she'd be able to solve the crime, get the Big Scoop, put the villain in jail and, not only get her summer job back, not only have a brilliant tale to tell back at school in the autumn, but also have a story worthy of winning the prestigious Prilchard-Spritzer Medal.

She glanced up at the framed copy of her parents' Last Will and Testament that hung on the kitchen wall.

It wasn't just about medals, although winning a medal would be one in the eye for the Head, who was always annoying Greta.* She also wanted to do right by her mum and dad. She didn't need to reread the important bit of the Last Will; she'd learnt it by heart a long time ago: *Greta, darling, try to find out as much stuff as you can. Knowledge is fun and useful. The world needs bright, inquisitive people like you to help it get by. Darling, be brilliant.*

And so she unwrapped the carrot cake she'd bought from Doodad's corner shop and put it on a plate.

* It wasn't just the banning her from being on the school newspaper that annoyed Greta. During the last school year she'd also been asked not to attend the after-school wrestling, origami and leopard-watching clubs, and had been sent home halfway through the school field trip to the Lake District for 'sarcastically commenting on the 'beautiful weather'.

She put the plate on the kitchen table.

She opened the kitchen window a couple of inches and hid herself in the empty breakfast cereal cupboard (she *knew* there'd been something else she'd meant to buy while in Doodad's).

And then Greta Zargo began her long wait.

CHAPTER TEN

Faddertyre VI

80 LIGHT YEARS FROM EARTH
8,912 YEARS AGO

THE BAR-TARRY-TUF PEOPLE of Faddertyre VI were one of the angriest species in the galaxy.

It wasn't that they were violent or war-like per se. It wasn't even that they argued with one another a lot. It wasn't as if their anger bubbled up to the surface from time to time with a roaring shout of rage and frustration even.

No. The Bar-Tarry-Tuffians never did any of that, because the Bar-Tarry-Tuffians never let on *just how angry they were*. None of them ever *said* anything. They had been brought up to be polite to one another and to not make a fuss. So they all smiled and just got on with their lives as if they were perfectly happy. But they weren't.

For example, when Filtash Quink was swimming lengths and Putnose Flarnk bellyflopped into the pool, making Quink breathe some unexpected water and lose count, the conversation went like this:

FQ, treading water, talking to himself: 'Blast. I've lost count of the number of lengths I've swum. Was it one hundred and seventeen or one hundred and eighteen? Oh blow, I'm just going to have to start again.'

PF, seeing Quink and swimming over: 'Hey, Quink! Did I splash you? Soz, mate.'

FQ, happily: 'No problem, Flarnk. I needed the exercise. Ha ha!'

PF, swimming off, noisily: 'Jolly good, buddy.'

FQ, shouting after PF: 'No worries. It's all good. Have a nice day, friend.'

FQ, inside: *Grrrrrrrrrrrrr.*

And then one day a silvery robot descended from the sky and landed in the city square, in amongst a whole crowd of Bar-Tarry-Tuffians.

'Take me to your leader,' it said in a calm, friendly metallic voice.

'Leader?' they said.

'Yes,' the machine said. 'Please take me to your leader.'

As the robot spoke, something strange happened.

The crowd of Bar-Tarry-Tuffians found themselves thinking, *Why on Faddertyre VI does the robot want to see him?*

Glaunch Wedfarc had only recently been elected Notwash. *Wedfarc is an incompetent imbecile*, they thought. *Not only does he have* three widdlepaps* *and that weird orange glumble-floam*★*, but he tilts his head-lobe to the left in a*

* A widdlepap is a bit like a spunion, but typically a slightly different shade of quelch, much longer and used for fallshappling rather than follshippling.

★ A glumblefloam is simply another name for an ilfbelp.

really annoying way whenever he speaks. It's too much to stand. Just too much!

'You don't want to see him,' said one Bar-Tarry-Tuffian. 'He's an idiot.'

The other Bar-Tarry-Tuffians looked at the Bar-Tarry-Tuffian who had just spoken her mind to this robotic visitor and they were amazed. Their speaking tubes flopped with admiration (mixed with a seething anger at the fact that *they* hadn't said it first).

'Nevertheless,' said the robot, 'it is my desire to speak to your leader.'

'He's a jerk,' whispered another Bar-Tarry-Tuffian, with a secret thrill.

'A right pimbledot,' said a third, blushingly.*

'He's a disgrace to the name of Wedfarc. My uncle was called Wedfarc and he was

* *A pimbledot is a fruit that smells a bit like a Bar-Tarry-Tuffian's second elbow joint.*

wonderful. How dare the Notwash go around with the same name as my uncle! What a grippit!'*

The voices were getting angrier.

What had happened? What was going on? No one had ever spoken like this before.

There was something about this visitor, this stranger, this thing from beyond Faddertyre VI, this outsider, that made them feel, for once, they didn't need to *hide their feelings*, that made them feel that, for the first time in their lives, they could open up and tell the truth and they wouldn't be judged for it.

And it felt *so good*.

The silvery robot didn't judge them. It didn't tut or humph or look disappointed; it just floated there looking silvery and

* A grippit is a small unsatisfying meal, only eaten while on a small unsatisfying holiday.

robotic, listening to whatever they wanted to say.

When reports of what was happening in that distant city square reached the Notwash's office, the Notwash was furious, absolutely fuming. How dare they, the people for whom he worked his flippers to the nub every day ... how dare they say such awful, hurtful things about him? It was absolutely unfair and unheard of. His emotions bubbled inside him like molten lava in a shoddily constructed volcano.

'It's a very pretty day today, lovely sunshine. Very warm and pleasant,' he said to Gufftog, his assistant.

When the robot arrived in the Notwash's office five minutes later, it said, 'Please may we have your planet?' as usual, unaware of the disturbance it had been causing.

Wedfarc Glaunch, the Notwash of Faddertyre VI, looked at this strange metal thing from beyond the world of the Bar-Tarry-Tuffians and felt the same loosening of good manners that the others had experienced in the city square.

He looked at the robot floating there in mid-air, all silvery and with little flashing lights, and realised that this thing probably didn't care about etiquette and not hurting anyone else's feelings. It was a messenger from beyond and it just wanted to know the truth.

'Please may we have your planet?' it asked again.

Wedfarc thought about all the irritating Bar-Tarry-Tuffians he had met during his lifetime and about the annoying shade of blue the sky always insisted on being.

He thought about the noise Gufftog made when she chewed yaffle* and about how you could never get fresh sadboll* in the city.

He thought about the way it always rained when he'd forgotten his hat, but never when he remembered it, and how all the Bar-Tarry-Tuffians he passed on the way to his office had *four* widdlepaps.

The volcano that had sat dormant but bubbling inside him for his entire life finally burst and he said, shouted almost, 'Goodness, yes! Take the planet! Take it all! Good luck to you, silvery robot-thing!'

And he ripped off his clothes and rolled on the floor in utter, sheer pleasure, burbling to himself and saying all the things he'd never been able to say before.

* *Yaffle is a thick porridge-like drink, made from the juice extracted from pimbledots. By the time it has been made into yaffle, the smell has mostly gone.*

★ *Sadboll looks almost exactly like the Earth plant spinach, but tastes almost exactly like lipplopp juice. It is prized by Bar-Tarry-Tuffians because no one enjoys squeezing lipplopps to get the juice out, especially not the lipplopps.*

Faddertyre VI is not there any more.

CHAPTER ELEVEN

Upper Lowerbridge, England, Earth

LAST THURSDAY, TEATIME

IT TOOK GRETA a few moments to work out where she was.

It was dark and warm in the cupboard.

She'd been asleep.

She pushed the door open and carefully climbed out.

On the kitchen table there was a plate but ... no cake.

'Blast it,' she said.

She'd missed the thief, when they'd struck in *her own house* in the very trap she'd set to catch them. If only that cupboard hadn't been so dark and warm, and if only the thief hadn't taken so long.

She examined the plate to see if there were any clues.

A few crumbs and a couple of little spiky muddy smears on the wood of the table.

Were *they* clues?

The crumbs were from the carrot cake — she was sure of that — but what was the mud?

She looked over at the kitchen window.

On the lip of the sink, which was set into the countertop just below the window, were a few more muddy marks.

Greta had left the window open just a few inches and it didn't seem to be open much further now.

She looked closer.

There *were* more crumbs there, carroty ones, but there was something else too.

Snagged on the window frame were a few tufty hairs.

Getting a pair of tweezers from her bedroom she picked them off the frame and dropped them into an envelope for safe keeping.

They were grey.

So, she thought, the Upper Lowerbridge Cake Thief had grey hair. Or, more correctly: the Upper Lowerbridge Cake Thief was *missing* some grey hair.

This was the first clue that actually gave her something solid to look for: *a small person*

missing some grey hair. How many people could that be? How many people could she now eliminate from her enquiries? Loads, probably.

And then, as she was examining her thoughts, she heard a noise. Outside.

She pulled the back door open and something moved, knocking over a flowerpot and darting away.

She caught only a fleeting glimpse of the person who'd run (they'd definitely been short and grey), but by the time Greta reached the edge of the patio, they'd already leapt over the hole at the far end of the garden and scrabbled across the great mound of earth beyond it, over the top and out of sight.

It *had* been the thief.

There were crumbs all over the patio. Some of them quite big.

What sort of person with grey hair could move like that? The thief had run at speed, bouncing along, and with one swift jump had leapt the hole. With almost supernatural nimbleness, they had got away.

If only she'd been quicker and had got a better look at them.

There'd been something else weird about the thief; she was sure of that. It had looked as if they'd been wearing a huge furry backpack. Old people (those with grey hair) didn't often wear great big fluffy backpacks, she thought, or run so fast.

Maybe the thief was a grey-haired kid?

Greta ran through a mental list of all the kids in her school and none of them had grey hair, and most of them were taller than the thief anyway. The Great Upper Lowerbridge Cake Thief (which was what she thought she'd call them in the paper) had been *very* short.

It was frustrating.

Next time she'd just have to be smarter, quicker, sharper.

Would the thief fall for a second trap if she laid one? It seemed unlikely. Maybe she'd just have to wait for someone else's cake to go missing? How could she work out where the thief would strike next?

It was then that something Jessica had said the other day popped into her mind like a tiny memory-shaped balloon: there was to be a party. She'd said something about tin foil.

Unable to remember any more, Greta jumped the low fence in between her garden and that of Brigadier Ryefoot-fforwerd (Rtd*), who lived next door, scooted across his lawn (as he stood on his patio and shouted at her, shaking his stick and turning red★) and jumped the fence on the other side.

'Jessica,' she shouted.

A window on the first floor of the house in whose garden Greta now stood opened and Jessica stuck her head out.

'Hi, Greta,' she said. 'I was just about to have a biscuit.'

* 'Rtd' is an abbreviation of the word 'retired', which means he's no longer in the army, not that he's recently had new air-filled rubber bits fitted to his wheels.

★ Brigadier Ryefoot-fforwerd only had three volumes: shouting, snoring and silence. The third of these could very occasionally be heard in the small gaps between the other two.

'That's OK,' said Greta. 'You said something about a party?' *

'It's at the Cohens' house, Friday night.'

'Will there be cake?'

'There's always cake at the Cohens' parties, Greta. Don't you remember last year when Sophie Doodad ate too much and fell in the pond?'

'Oh yes,' said Greta, 'of course.'

She remembered the chocolate cake, which had had a horrible coffee cream in the middle of it. She also remembered there were an awful lot of other cakes there too. Would the cake thief be able to resist so many cakes all in one place? Unlikely.

'What are you going as?' Jessica asked.

But Greta was too busy thinking about finally catching the thief to hear the question.

* Clause nineteen of Greta's parents' Last Will and Testament said, Greta, darling, do try to attend as many fancy dress parties as possible, especially those held by our near neighbours, the Cohens. It wasn't Greta's favourite bit of the will. She found parties a bit confusing, all those people expecting you to say things to them.

114

'I've got to go,' she said, as she jumped back over the low fence and headed home.

'Goodbye,' said Jessica, waving at her best friend and listening to Brigadier Ryefoot-fforwerd (Rtd) shouting. She made a note of some of the more colourful language in the special glittery notebook she kept for vocabularial purposes.

CHAPTER TWELVE

Belf-Trooga

4.3 LIGHT YEARS FROM EARTH
438 YEARS AGO

T HE SMALL, FURRY creatures that inhabited the planet Belf-Trooga had found the journey to civilisation to be a long and difficult one.

The main cause of difficulty was that Belf-Trooga was a windy planet and the Belf-Troogans were a small and furry people. Fire is an essential stepping stone on the path across the river of progress, but when you are small and furry and the weather's windy, fire isn't always your friend.

As it happened, fire was actually discovered *many* times by *many* different Belf-Troogans over the millennia. Most Belf-Troogans who witnessed the discovery of fire by a fellow Belf-Troogan (a) vowed never to discover fire themselves, because it looked noisy, hot and painful, and (b) ate tasty, freshly cooked meat for the first time in their small, furry lives.

Eventually a Belf-Troogan called Feefal, who took the bold step of growing so old that she went bald, plucked a blazing branch from a lightning-struck tree and didn't immediately burst into flames herself. Instead she poked several long-haired verfell-hogs with the burning stick and watched as they became juicy, flavoursome and calorifically rich meals.

And so it was that Feefal finally set her people on the long road to civilisation, and now, several thousand years later, Belf-Trooga was a planet on its way up.

Glorious shining cities reached for the skies and glorious shining ships sailed the oceans. Belf-Troogans had even ventured into space, sending back photos of amusingly shaped asteroids, and there was a general feeling of optimism in the air. Belf-Trooga was a planet at peace with enough food for everyone; skateboards were back in fashion and a new series of *Once a Deptrok, Always a Deptrok* was beginning in the autumn. Ah, but it was bliss to be alive in those times.

And then, as if from nowhere, a strange

silvery robot landed in the main square of Belf-Trooga's main city, Belt-Nagling.

'Take me to your leader,' it said.

'We all lead,' said a surprised, passing Belf-Troogan. 'This is a democracy. Look, here is my voting pod.'

From underneath its fur it produced a little device with glowing buttons. Every few minutes the voting pod would buzz and a question would appear on the little screen and the Belf-Troogans would press the appropriate button and the votes of the whole race would be tallied up by a giant computer that would then make something happen.

In centuries past, long and desperate wars had been fought in the name of democracy, and now, finally, it was here in its truest form and at last everyone felt included, felt a part of the system. Everyone's vote was counted and every vote counted. No one was left out.

The voting pod buzzed and the Belf-Troogan talking to the robot said, 'Excuse me a moment,' read the question ('Should ziffgubs be blue or green this week?'), pressed one of the pod's buttons ('Blue') and turned back to the robot.

'You are the leader?' the robot asked.

'Yes. As much as anyone,' said the Belf-Troogan.

'Very well. Please may we have your planet?'

The Belf-Troogan's fur fluffed like a startled krowt-pip.

'Pardon?' it said, just to make sure it had heard right.

'Please may we have your planet?'

However polite the question had been, the Belf-Troogan didn't like it. Its species had spent thousands of years living through *history*, not always happily, not always easily. And now some silvery robot from outer space just turned up and asked to *have* the planet? The hard sacrifices made by generations of Belf-Troogans to ensure their offspring would finally know democracy and daylight and skateboards bubbled inside the small, furry creature. No shiny silver robot was going to take that away from them.

'Over my dead body,' it said, pulling itself up to its small height and rippling its fur in an aggressive manner.

The silvery robot lifted up in the air and whirred as it double-checked its language banks. It didn't want to make a mistake.

'Thank you,' it said, and, opening a little hatch in its side, extended a painless death ray towards the Belf-Troogan, who collapsed in a painless dead heap.

One problem with robots is, of course, their habit of taking everything at face value; that is to say that they always assume people are telling them the truth. They don't recognise nuance and metaphor, subtlety and delicacy, tiptoeing and sidestepping in a language, that is to say, wordplay and poetry, smoke and mirrors, cheekiness and talking round the houses, and so you should always be careful and clear when speaking to them. If you mean no, just say 'no'.

Within the hour a fleet of silvery robots had completed their survey of the planet and the more destructive robots had begun their syphoning, storing, dismantling and recycling work.

No amount of pressing the 'Ask the Death Robots from Outer Space to Leave'

CHAPTER THIRTEEN

Upper Lowerbridge, England, Earth

LAST FRIDAY, BREAKFAST-TIME

FRIDAY MORNING ARRIVED at about eight o'clock and Greta woke up.

She normally went to visit her grandads, Jasper and Zoltan Zargo, on a Friday. (She caught the bus in the morning during the holidays, or after school during the not-holidays.)

Once upon a time they'd worked in a travelling circus, and Aunt Tabitha said they argued so much because they missed the old circus days. She also said she was working on a rejuvenating machine that would allow them to regain their youthful physiques and return to the wandering showbiz life, because their neighbours complained to her about the noise whenever she went to visit. But rejuvenation is difficult and the machine was still not yet ready.

Grandad Zoltan had once been The Great Zargo, a human cannonball who would sing 'Happy Birthday' to a member of the audience as he flew through the air. If there were very many people with birthdays on the same day he would perform the act very many times, not always to the joy of people without birthdays who'd come along to the circus to see the dancing dogs and sword swallowers and flaming hoops and all the rest.

Grandad Jasper had worked behind the scenes, oiling the cannon, cooking Zoltan's meals and sewing sequins on to his leotard. *
He didn't mind this; after all, he blushed whenever people looked at him and enjoyed the smell of fresh oil. Circus life wasn't so bad.

Today, however, Greta didn't have time to go visit them. There were things she needed to do before the party.

'Hello,' said a creaky voice at the other end of the telephone.

'Grandad Jasper,' Greta said. 'I won't be visiting today. I've got things I need to do. See you next week.'

'Greta,' said Grandad Jasper. 'Is that you, love?'

'Yes,' said Greta, louder and slower. 'I can't come visit today.'

* Being fired from a cannon was one of the main causes of lost sequins in the latter part of the twentieth century, just behind crocodile attacks and sudden bouts of overeating.

'Don't worry, love,' her grandad said. 'Bertie Rustle's come to see us, so there wouldn't be a chair for you anyway.

Maybe we'll see you tonight? At the party?'

'Maybe,' she said.

So, they were coming to the party too, were they?

Five minutes later Greta was once again on Jessica's patio.

'Jessica,' she shouted.

An upstairs window opened and Jessica stuck her head out.

(The noise of the shouting ex-Brigadier in the garden next door filled the gaps between their words as they spoke.)

'Hi, Greta,' Jessica said. 'If you wait there I'll be down in a minute. We can go play up the park; it's a lovely day.'

'Tell me more about the party,' Greta said. 'What did you say the theme is? Is it fruit again?'

The year before it had been 'fruits of the world', to celebrate the hundredth anniversary of the melon.*

'Oh no. This time it's space. I didn't even know it was the sixtieth anniversary of the moon landing until I got the

* Jessica Plumb had gone as a plum. It had been very funny. People kept asking her, 'What are you, Plumb?' and she'd say, 'Yes'. Oh, how everyone laughed. Greta hadn't laughed as much as everyone else, however, since she'd dressed as a banananana and had got stuck in a doorway for several hours. (The banananana was one of Aunt Tabitha's creations, designed for hungry people who only had time to peel one piece of fruit. It was twice as long as the old-fashioned banana, and an improvement of several inches on her previous effort, the bananana.)

132

invitation. I'm such a silly.' *

'Space. OK,' said Greta. 'Thanks.'

'Shall we go up the park?' asked Jessica. 'We could play football or throw sticks at ducks or …'

But Greta didn't hear. She was too busy thinking about what to do for her costume, and had already reached and opened her front door and gone inside and taken her shoes off and climbed upstairs.

It needed to blend in perfectly with the theme of the party, but also allow her the perfect opportunity to catch the thief when she saw him or her lay a finger on the cakes.

Her first thought was to go as a Space Scone. But where would she get Space Flour and Space Eggs and Space Sugar on a Friday? They weren't the sorts of things

* BASA (British Agency of Space Adventures) had launched the Boudica 8 from Ventnor Spaceport sixty years ago that summer. Bernice Wickett's iconic first words, 'Oops, mind that step, Graham,' will be remembered for as long as human beings remember them.

Sophie Doodad had in her corner shop.

What about a Space Monster that could shoot glue out from its eyes? That would be perfect for catching a thief. The moment she saw a cake move it would be *squirt!* Eye-glue all over the villain ...

But as far as she knew there was no such thing as eye-glue, and Aunt Tabitha probably wouldn't have time to invent it.

This was difficult.

It would require more thought than a normal Friday morning had room for, so Greta ran herself a bubble bath with *extra* bubbles and made herself a Marmite sandwich.

Then she sank beneath the steamy suds, nibbled and began to think extra hard.

* * *

When Greta resurfaced, the water was cold, the sandwich soggy and the answer was in her head.

She had a blue T-shirt and a cap with the BASA logo on. She'd go as one of the people from mission control. It wasn't exactly pushing the boat out so far as exciting costumes went, but it would do, especially because it meant she'd be carrying a butterfly net.*
That would come in really handy.

But it wasn't just the ideal costume that had bubbled into her mind while she'd been thinking so hard; something else had gone *ping* as well. It was something Grandad Jasper had said.

He'd said that he and Grandad Zoltan had a visitor: Bertie Rustle.

The name hadn't meant anything at first, but while she was in the bath a memory

* The butterfly net had become the unofficial symbol of BASA after the moon landing because of the issue they'd had with all the butterflies (and other insects, hummingbirds and geese) who mistook the colourful computer screens in mission control for a beeping floral display. Just as Wickett and Stump had been about to touch down on the moon.

136

had popped into her head.

Bertie Rustle was short for Bertram Rustle and Bertram Rustle had been a shorter-than-average contortionist and acrobat her grandads had worked with back in the circus. He had been famous for squeezing himself through holes that less flexible people couldn't fit through. Audiences had fallen off the edge of their seats watching him. It had been years since she'd seen him round her grandads' house, but she remembered he'd been quite small and old back then. Now? Well, now he must be even smaller and older, and Grandad Jasper had confirmed that Rustle was in the area. Right now.

What did she know about the thief? What had she learnt from her own investigations? It was this: the thief was a tiny person with grey hair who could move fast and climb through tight windows with ease.

Bertram Rustle loved cake. Greta remembered Grandad Zoltan saying so once. Rustle had visited a few years ago on a Thursday, and when she'd made her usual Friday visit her grandad had greeted her at the door by saying, 'There's no cake left, love. Never is when Bertie's been to visit.'

What more was there to say?

All she had to do now was catch Rustle in the act of nicking a cake from the party and the case would be closed, the mystery solved and she'd be able to write the story up ready for the front page of the newspaper.

Except, of course, it wouldn't be on the front page of the newspaper because Mr Inglebath had sacked her, because he preferred to do what Mrs Hummock, his sister-in-law, said, instead of being dedicated heart and soul to The Truth like what she was.

Well, she'd use the photocopier in the library and just make her own newspaper, as Aunt Tabitha had suggested. It would still be something to leave on the Head's desk when they went back to school. It would still be a pretty cool thing that nobody could deny: *Greta Zargo, crime solver! Greta Zargo, winner!*

It might still be Prilchard-Spritzer-Medal-worthy, even if she published it herself. It was *such* a good story.

Greta had to admit, she was brilliant.

CHAPTER FOURTEEN

Middling Otherbridge, England, Earth

LAST SUNDAY

THE SILVERY ROBOT landed beside a low building.

'Take me to your leader,' it said to the world at large, assuming that if someone were within hearing range they would answer.

'Go see The Great Zargo,' said a voice.

The robot swivelled and focused its camera-eyes.

Through a window it could see a biolo-gical life form sat on a soft rectangular structure.* It had two arm-limbs and two leg-limbs and a ball with what appeared to be various sense organs protruding from the top of a barrel-shaped body.*

*It was a bed.
*It was a human.

The robot had seen others of this type around. *They must be*, it computed, *the dominant species on this planet.* They were featured, after all, in many of the television programmes it had watched in order to learn English from as it approached the planet.

'Take me to your leader,' it repeated.

The figure scratched under one of the arm-limbs with the little mini-limbs at the end of the opposite arm-limb, but it didn't speak.

'Go see The Great Zargo,' said the voice that had spoken before.

A metal cage hung in the corner of the room. In it a colourful animal, about the size of a squawlk-gurd from the third moon of Trixl-Dar, sat on a wooden perch. *

'Go see The Great Zargo?' the robot repeated.

'Go see The Great Zargo,' the parrot confirmed.

'Very well,' said the silvery robot, already lifting up into the sky.

Robots, it should be remembered, as has been mentioned before, are amongst the most trusting things in the universe. They do not understand irony, sarcasm or metaphor*. They always tell the truth and always assume they are being told the truth. They are, in fact, the exact opposite of cats.

As it flew the robot probed the internet to discover the location of this 'Great Zargo', leader of the people of the planet Earth.

The first relevant entry it discovered was Greta Zargo's birth certificate, on which her father had made a minor spelling mistake.

Another seven seconds of searching through the computerised records of the Earth turned up an address.

* For a fuller list of the figures of speech and turns of phrase robots don't understand see paragraph one on page 125.

144

Birth Certificate

This Certifies That

Great Zargo
(Name)

Was born

On Tuesday   At Lunch
    (Date)   (Time)

Middling Otherbridge
         (Location)

It was only a few miles from where the robot had first landed.

Course was set for the town of Upper Lowerbridge.

*   *   *

Back in the bedroom, Zoltan Zargo was shouting at his parrot.

'Shut up, Bertha. I'm tryin' a think. Between you and the radio and that metal thing outside, I can't remember what I came in here for.'

'Go see The Great Zargo,' the parrot repeated.

'If only,' the once-Great Zargo said. 'But I ain't feelin' so great no more.'

Bertha preened under her wing and then ate a peanut.

She had been with Zoltan Zargo for fifty years and the only thing she'd ever learnt to say had been that one phrase, the phrase that would draw eager customers into the Big Top night after night. Well, that and 'Bertha wants a cracker', but she wasn't hungry just then. *

* She'd just had a peanut, after all.

CHAPTER FIFTEEN

Upper Lowerbridge, England, Earth

LAST FRIDAY, TEATIME

GRETA WAS ON the pavement outside the Cohens' house, watching the guests arrive. She made a note in her head of what people were wearing, as if she were a reporter on the red carpet of some swanky movie premiere.

The Merridews from number sixteen, the Appledumps from number twenty-five and Mr Borris from opposite Greta's house had all dressed as the aliens from the *Don't Mind Me, I'm Your Mother* series of films*, and were arguing on the front lawn.

Belinda Archangel, the soprano who lived in the flat above Sophie Doodad's shop, had wound tin foil around herself and was humming the famous aria from Wingstein's opera *Space Mummy versus the World*.

Brigadier Ryefoot-fforwerd (Rtd) was wearing his old army uniform with all his medals on, which didn't really count as fancy dress, but since he wasn't very nice and shouted a lot, no one complained, because that would have meant spending time with him.

Aunt Tabitha arrived on a floating bicycle she'd invented, just like the one that Janet Weatherfall rode in *Which Way to the Future?*

* *Don't Mind Me, I'm Your Mother* (2008), *Don't Mind Me, I'm Your Mother Too* (2011), *Remind Me, Who's Your Mother?* (2012), *Return of the Son of Your Mother* (2015), *Whose Mother Am I Anyway?* (2016), *I'm Your Mother VI: This Time it's Your Dad* (2018), and *Don't Mind Me, I'm Not Your Mother, But I Knew Her Well, Once, Several Years Ago* (2023).

But even though everyone was impressed, Greta could see that there was a hint of sadness in the corner of her aunt's left eye.

'What is it, Auntie?' she asked.

'Jonathon still hasn't come home. I do so worry for him,' her aunt replied.

'Oh dear,' Greta said.

She didn't have to comfort her sad aunt for long, because just then her Grandad Jasper arrived, dressed as a Space Pirate, with a little grey Space Monkey waddling beside him.

'Grandad Zoltan's still under the weather, love,' he told Greta. 'He's stayed at home.' He leaned in close. 'Between you and me, though,' he whispered, 'I think he just didn't want to miss *Dance, Baker, Dance!*'

'Where did you get a Space Monkey from?' Greta asked.

'Oh, it's not a real Space Monkey,' her grandad said. 'It's just Bert in fancy dress. Go on, give her a twirl, Bert.'

And the Space Monkey twirled, and Greta saw that it was indeed Bertram Rustle, the shorter-than-average, elderly but sprightly circus performer she'd been waiting for. (He wasn't wearing the strange big furry back-pack she'd seen him with before, but that wasn't surprising, since monkeys, even space ones, rarely wear backpacks.)

Aha! she thought, nevertheless.

'He's been staying with us this week while his bungalow is moved a bit further to the right,' her grandad explained. 'It'll get more sunshine, he reckons, when it's done.'

She wanted to slap her hand down on Rustle's shoulder and say, 'Someone call for the police and a photographer. I have captured the infamous Upper Lowerbridge Cake Thief.' But there was no point.

All the evidence she had and all the suspicions she held would only add up if she caught the thief red-handed. Until then it would just be her word against his, and almost everybody trusted elderly circus performers more than they trusted eleven-year-old girls.

She had to be patient.

She tried hard to not stare, because she didn't want Rustle to know she was on to him.

Patience, Greta, she thought, *patience*, as she watched them all go into the house.

Ten minutes later she was in the Cohens' kitchen watching the cakes. *

Watching them carefully.

Watching them closely.

(Her butterfly net was held ready.)

There were an awful lot of cakes. More than enough to prove irresistible to a hungry old man.

She just had to wait.

She edged back into a dark corner of the kitchen and stood still. She imagined she was playing musical statues and the music had stopped, which was something she'd never

* The party was fancy dress and the cakes were too. There were cakes shaped like rockets and planets and aliens and amusingly shaped asteroids. In the centre of the table was the largest cake of all, made to look like an exact model of the Boudica 8's landing module, The Henry, the module that had taken Bernice Wickett and Graham Stump to the surface of the moon all those years ago.

154

done, not having been invited to those sorts of parties very often.

She was, however, a very determined, recently sacked, investigative-reporter-cum-schoolgirl.

Twenty-two minutes went by before anything interesting happened.

And even then the interesting thing that happened was just that Jessica Plumb found her and said, 'Hi, Greta. Have you seen Sophie Doodad? She's got the most wonderful robot costume. It's all silver and has flashing lights and everything. I'm very jealous. Do you like my outfit?'

Jessica twirled.

She looked like a plum, with extra tin foil.

'I'm the Carnivorous Plumulon from *Space Adventures in Space*, series two, episode thirty-six,' she said excitedly.

Greta had only seen the first series of *Space Adventures in Space*, so she said, 'Very good. I'm on a mission, Jessica. Go away for a bit.'

Jessica, recognising that her best friend was involved in some serious business that she'd probably find out about later on, nodded and went away. (She didn't mind. There were other people she could show her costume off to, and there were seven different flavours of crisps in bowls in seven different rooms around the house, and she thought that by eating two, or possibly three, crisps from different bowls *at the same time* she might be able to invent some new flavours. She secretly wanted to be an inventor like Greta's aunt, but her parents were still alive and annoying, so she had hardly invented anything yet.)

Greta went on watching from under the brim of her baseball cap.

Sixteen minutes later and still all the cakes were unstolen.*

'Ladies and gentlemen, boys and girls,

* *Except for the stollen, which was almost stolen. (This is a spelling-related joke, regarding a rich fruit-and-nut loaf of German origin, the English word 'stolen' and the letter 'l'.)*

spacemen and spacewomen,' shouted Mrs Cohen, tinging a fork on the side of a glass. 'Let us repair to the street, where Mr Cohen and I will recreate the moment we are all here to remember, the landing of *The Henry*, and the historic descent of Wickett and Stump to the moon's surface.'

Greta had seen the full-size model of the lunar module dangling from a large crane in the street as she'd arrived and had, at first, wondered what it was for. But when she'd seen Mr and Mrs Cohen in their replica BASA space suits, it had all become clear. They really did go to a lot of effort for their parties.

Everyone began filing out of the house into the street.

Everyone except Greta.

She was willing to miss the re-enactment.

With everyone gone, now was the obvious time for the thief to strike. She couldn't risk missing it.

But she needed a better hiding place. Just standing stock-still like a statue in the shadowy corner of the kitchen wasn't good enough, she decided.

She quickly looked around and found the biggest cupboard. After moving all the brooms, buckets, mops, boxes of moth balls and clothes pegs, detergent, coats and gardening gloves, dustpans and brushes, old rope and boxes of dog biscuits and fish food, bird seed and candlesticks, candles and roadmaps of Scotland, minor Impressionist paintings of negligible worth and umbrellas, umbrellas and more umbrellas carefully aside, she climbed in.

And as she did so, pulling the door

half-shut behind her, she heard a noise from the kitchen.

The soft spongy noise of a cake being purloined.

She leapt out, butterfly net slamming down on the big table, splatting the icing on one alien-planet-shaped cake and knocking a Swiss roll in the shape of a rocket over …

… but the thief was too quick for her.

A grey shape yelped and darted out the window, leaving a cloud of icing sugar, currants and crumbs behind it.

Greta ran for the back door, which was open, trailing cake debris behind her as the large hoop of the butterfly net banged into, and sent flying, more delicious articles of party food. *

And then she was out on the patio, and the thief was in front of her.

* Crisps, peanuts, cakes, two truckles of cheese, strudel, cakes, various dips, various cakes, sausage rolls, carrot sticks, pickled dormice, unpickled cakes, chocolate buttons, dried apricots, cakes and juicy pineapple cubes, to be precise.

He was hunched underneath the garden table, nibbling the edge of a large hunk of Victoria sponge, jammy filling spurting out and crumbs flying everywhere.

He was definitely small and grey and hairy, just like the Space-Monkey-cum-elderly-circus-performer she'd seen earlier, and he had his back to her.

He was sat in the shadows under the table, but she could see that he was wearing the same strange-looking, loose-flapping furry backpack she'd seen the day before. This made her pause for a moment, since the old man hadn't been wearing it when he arrived, but maybe, she thought, as her brain hurtled through possibilities, it was his lucky thieving backpack and he'd only just put it back on when he went for the cake. That made sense, sort of.

'I've got you now, Rustle,' Greta shouted as she swooped the hoop of the butterfly net between the table legs and over the thief's head.

But he had already darted away.

Oh! His reactions were fast for an old man.

But it turned out Greta's had actually been even quicker. She was yanked forwards as the cake thief ran off – *she'd caught him!*

He was writhing, tugging at the butterfly net, and it was all she could do to keep a grip on the handle. The grey fur of Rustle's Space Monkey costume poked through the fine holes of the net in tiny fluffy patches as he wriggled and struggled.

Then, with a vigorous tug, Greta was pulled off the patio and hauled up the garden.

The thief was moving slowly, with great effort, huffing and puffing and squeaking and muttering, still wrapped up in the net, dragging Greta across the lawn behind him.

'Grrr!' said Greta, gripping hard on the handle. 'Why don't you just stop? There's no point fighting! I've got you now!'

She fought to keep hold of the net as she slid across the grass on her belly.

And then something unexpected happened.

A large silvery shape descended from the sky, with a slow, quiet whoosh of unknown energy, and settled on the lawn beside her.

'Are you The Great Zargo?' the thing asked.

Greta grunted a 'Yes, yes'. She wasn't really paying attention to the silvery shape, and only half heard the words.

The handle of the butterfly net slipped out of her hand, but the thief was all tangled up. He began hopping and staggering across the lawn, towards the woods at the end of the garden. He made slow progress.

'Grrr!' she said again, climbing to her feet, burbling with frustration.

She went to chase after him, but the silvery robot floated in front of her.

'Out of my way,' she said, attempting to get past it.

'Please may we have your planet?' the thing said.

'What?' she snapped, leaning round and watching the struggling and slowly rolling shape in the net.

Rustle was getting away and this floating silver robot was asking her stupid questions.

And then she remembered what Jessica

had said: Sophie Doodad was dressed as a robot with flashing lights.

'Mind out, Sophie,' Greta said, stepping round the robot, which hovered back into her way with a floaty movement. She added a quick 'please' to the 'mind out', because Sophie preferred people to be polite.

It was a good costume, she'd give Sophie that much.

'Please may we have your planet?'

'No, of course you can't,' Greta said distractedly. (The thief had almost reached the trees. She thought he was almost out of the net too. Her Big Scoop was getting away. She didn't have time for this.) 'Look, I'm sorry, Sophie, I'm in a bit of a hurry.'

And Greta pushed past the silvery, floating robot and ran towards the far end of the garden.

'Very well. Sorry to have bothered you,' the robot said calmly, smoothly, as it drifted up into the sky behind her with a slow, quiet whoosh of unknown energy.*

* Greta Zargo just saved the world. In case you missed it. That was it. Sometimes it doesn't take much, just someone to say no, but still she deserves our thanks. She saved us all. Well done, Greta.

CHAPTER SIXTEEN

High Earth Orbit

LAST FRIDAY, SEVENTEEN MINUTES LATER

THE THING ABOUT robots, as has been mentioned several times before, is that they're very literal-minded.

They'd asked for the planet, and the leader of the people of the planet had said no.

So that was that.

Fair enough.

Simple.

The silvery robot approached the Huge

Space-Going Robot and informed it of the Earthlings' leader's decision.

The Huge Space-Going Robot examined its databanks for instructions. Computers whirred and computed deep inside its enormous electronic brain and fourteen seconds later a new course of action was plotted and shared between the two robots.

Vast engines glowed with unknown energy at the rear of the Huge Space-Going one and its sweeping sensors scanned the sky for a nearby star to set course for.

(The much smaller silvery robot quickly got out of its way with its usual quiet whoosh.)

Slowly the Huge Space-Going Robot left the Earth, and the rest of the solar system, behind.

Onward and outward it flew on its ongoing mission of exploration.

The small silvery robot placed itself into an unobtrusive orbit, tilted one of its antennae in the direction of Cestrypip, 965 light years away towards the constellation of Cygnus, and began to retransmit a continuous stream of Earthling television.

Episodes of *Babies Break Antiques* and *Marry My Mother, Maybe* and *Dance, Baker, Dance* travelled out across the galaxy, to be deciphered, analysed and entered into the chapter on Earth in the *Harknow-Bumfurly-Histlock Big Book of Galactic Facts*™.

CHAPTER SEVENTEEN

Upper Lowerbridge, England, Earth

STILL LAST FRIDAY

GRETA LANDED ON the handle of the butterfly net with a clatter.

It was a spectacular dive.

She dragged it towards her, the wriggling shape of the grey-haired contortionist inside still not quite free of the netting.

'Got you!' she shouted triumphantly.

She pulled it nearer.

Now that she'd got a bit closer she noticed that the wriggling shape seemed a bit small, even for an elderly contortionist, but it *was* grey and furry, and it did look a *bit* like a Space Monkey, so who else could it be?

Oh, she thought, disappointedly.

Between the cake crumbs and fluttering fur she saw she'd actually caught a squirrel. A very large squirrel, but a squirrel none-theless.

As Greta Zargo approached the house, the giant squirrel still bundled up in the net but not struggling so much now, she thought about how she'd tell the story, how she'd describe the way the clues had added up, how she'd tracked the villain, how she'd saved the day and saved the cakes of Upper Lowerbridge forever.

(She didn't need to say how she'd got it wrong and almost accused an innocent old man; she could pretend she'd suspected a squirrel all along and no one would know any different.)

It was going to be a brilliant article. It would make the front page of *The Local Newspaper* for sure, if only ... Well, the library's photocopier would have to do ... It would still be brilliant, however she got the story out there.

The lunar landing re-enactment out in the street had finished and people were milling on the patio, eating sausage rolls and drinking cold drinks with a bright chink of ice cubes.

It was a warm, fresh summer's evening and everyone was laughing and smiling, except for Mr Cohen, who was shouting something or other about a frightful mess in the kitchen.

'Jonathon!' shouted Aunt Tabitha, rushing over to Greta.

'No, Auntie,' Greta said, slightly confused. 'I'm Greta.'

'No, silly,' her aunt said, at the purring netted bundle in Greta's hands.* 'That's Jonathon. You found him.'

Greta knew this big squirrel had seemed familiar; now everything fell into place.

'I didn't really *find* him,' she said. 'I *caught* him. You see … he's been responsible for all the cake thefts.'

'Not so loud, darling,' her aunt said, taking her by the elbow and leading her to one side.

They edged over to the ornamental pond.

'What do you mean, Jonathon's responsible?'

* *Aunt Tabitha had decided her giant vegetarian squirrel should purr, because it seemed like a good idea at the time.*

177

'Just that. All these thefts. It's been him every time.'

'Darling,' Aunt Tabitha said, concern in her hushed voice, 'how can you be sure? It really doesn't sound like him. He's allergic to peanuts, you know.'

Greta ran through the clues she'd found: the grey hairs, the scratchy, muddy marks on the table (that she now saw had been squirrel footprints), the small windows the thief had climbed through, the bouncy scampering she'd witnessed in her garden. Plus, and most damningly, she'd *caught him red-handedly stealing a cake not five minutes earlier*.

Aunt Tabitha couldn't deny that flood of evidence.

'Hello, hello, hello, what's all this then?' said Wilf Inglebath, coming over to where they were talking. 'Gossip, gossip, gossip. Folk talking where they can't be heard by a man of the press? Looks suspicious. Oh, hello, Greta.'

He hadn't realised who Tabitha was talking to when he came over, and so he blushed and blustered as he said Greta's name.

'Do you fancy a nut?' he said, and held out the little bowl of peanuts he'd been carrying.

'Mr Inglebath,' Greta said, ignoring the nuts, 'I've just caught the Great Upper Lowerbridge Cake Thief and I'm going to write up the story and it's going to be brilliant and every newspaper in the county's going to want to publish it.'

Aunt Tabitha tried to shush her, but Greta was carried away, the excitement of the moment and her achievement overtaking her.

'Oh,' said Mr Inglebath. 'Hmm. Er ...'

'Go on,' Greta said. 'Imagine this story on your front page. You've gotta take me back.'

'Well,' he said, obviously thinking about it.

Last week's headline had been: DOG CHASES STICK. And it hadn't even been an amusingly shaped stick.

'I'd love to, Greta,' he said. 'You were always my best reporter, ever since you first turned up with that story about the Lower

Upperbridge High School Marching Band's off-key rendition of the theme tune to the popular kids' show *Doughnuts & Dimples* a fortnight ago … but if Lucy ever found out, I'd never hear the end of it.'

(Lucy was another name for Mrs Hummock.)

Greta's aunt, who was holding the giant vegetarian squirrel in her arms and absent-mindedly stroking it, looked at her niece and at the sparkle in her eyes, and felt something in her own heart shiver happily. The joy Greta had got from solving the mystery was just the same as when Tabitha invented something new and wondrous. She understood that that sparkle deserved to be shared, front page and all.

'Wilf,' she said, turning to face the newspaperman. 'How would it be if Greta *apologised* to Mrs Hummock? Do you think you'd be able to take her back then?'

Mr Inglebath looked from the scientist to the schoolgirl and back again.

'Have you met Greta?' he said, suggesting with this simple phrase that the words 'Greta' and 'apology' were unlikely to be found in the same sentence in the wild.

Greta looked at her old editor's face. She looked at her aunt. She understood what needed to be done. She had to be the grown up. She had to suck in her pride and go and apologise to the rotten old trout. She could keep her fingers crossed when she did it and as long as Mrs Hummock didn't see … what would it matter?

'I could …' she said. 'I suppose I *could* apologise to Mrs Hummock. Is she here, Mr Inglebath?'

'Yes, she's over by the beehives,' he said, pointing at a woman dressed as a satellite. She was standing with another woman, her gossip partner, Mrs Wedlock, who was dressed as Mrs Wedlock. *

'Come on then,' said Greta.

Aunt Tabitha and Wilf Inglebath followed her across the lawn.

'Mrs Hummock,' said Greta when she arrived. 'I'd like to apologise for having said whatever it was I said to you the other day that upset you.'

'Um, Greta,' Aunt Tabitha said quietly. 'I'm not sure …'

'I'm *very* sorry. I shouldn't have said it. Whatever it was.'

Mrs Hummock stared open-mouthed and confused.

Mrs Wedlock tutted.

* Which actually qualified as a 'space-themed' outfit, since Mrs Wedlock had been the first person to orbit Venus. She didn't do that 'flying around in space' stuff any more, not since her hip had started playing up.

183

Once she'd gathered her wits and recognised exactly which little girl was talking to her, Mrs Hummock said, 'What are you on about?'

'It's an apology,' Greta said. 'I'm very sorry I said things when I was asking you about your cake.'

'Oh yes, the cake,' said Mrs Hummock.

Mrs Wedlock tutted.

Neither of them looked very impressed with the apology.

'Is that enough, Mr Inglebath?' Greta asked.

'Lucy,' Mr Inglebath said. 'Do say you forgive the girl. Then we can put it all behind us and get on with our lives, eh?'

'I remember now!' Mrs Hummock said, pulling her space-satellite-suited self up to her full height. 'She accused me of having

184

stolen my own cake. I will not forgive this … child.'

Mrs Wedlock tutted.

Greta looked from Mrs Hummock to Mr Inglebath to her aunt to Mrs Hummock to Mrs Wedlock to her aunt to Mrs Hummock to her aunt to Mr Inglebath to Mrs Hummock and finally just shrugged her shoulders.

'I tried,' she said.

There was an awkward silence as they all stood there, not sure who should speak next.

'Peanut?' said Mr Inglebath after a moment, once again proffering the little bowl he'd been carrying with him.

This time Greta took one and popped it in her mouth.

'Hang on!' she spurted, spitting peanut crumbs into the air.

She waved her finger and pointed it, accusingly, in Mrs Hummock's direction.

She'd just remembered something. Something that changed *everything*.

'I'm going to ask you a very simple question, Mrs H, and I want the truth. I want the facts.'

'Young lady, how dare you demand anything of me?' warbled Mrs Hummock.

Mrs Wedlock tutted.

'Greta, simmer down now,' said Mr Inglebath, trying to smooth the waters. 'We're all a bit tired and —'

'Look, I *know* who stole the cakes, Mrs Hummock. I know who stole them all. But Mr Socket's cake and Mr Teachbaddly's cake and my cake and the Cohens' cakes in there: they've all got something in common … something that makes *your* cake the odd one out.'

'I'm sure I don't know what you're talking about,' said Mrs Hummock, flustering.

'This is the squirrel that stole the cakes,' Greta said, pointing at the giant fluffy-tailed rodent in Aunt Tabitha's arms. 'Mrs Hummock,' she went on, 'tell us what *sort of* cake the cake you lost was?'

'I've had enough of this,' Mrs Hummock said and turned to walk away.

Mrs Wedlock tutted, and then turned to follow her friend.

Greta reached up to the lapel of her BASA Mission Control Operative's shirt and pressed the button on the badge labelled 'Press' that was pinned there.

There was a buzz and a crackle and then Mrs Hummock's voice rang out clearly from the badge's tiny speaker: 'It was a sponge,' the voice said, 'with peanut butter fondant icing. You see, Mrs Wedlock likes –'

Aunt Tabitha gasped.

Mrs Hummock and Mrs Wedlock stopped walking and turned to face the voice from the badge, which repeated itself several times on a loop.

'What is it, Tabs?' said Mr Inglebath.

'Tell him, Auntie.'

'Jonathon ...' Aunt Tabitha nodded at the squirrel that she was carrying (he was asleep and purring). 'He's mine,' she said. 'And he ... he's *allergic to peanuts*, the poor thing.'

'Aha!' shouted Greta, waving her finger

in the air triumphantly.

'What?' snapped Mrs Wedlock, turning on her friend.* 'You told me that the cake was stolen by the cake thief. When I asked why there were crumbs in your beard, you pointed at a picture of a tram to distract me. Now, I put it to you, Mrs Hummock, that you scoffed the cake before I got there.'

'Lucy,' said Mr Inglebath. 'Is this all true?'

Mrs Hummock looked ashamed. She looked shocked. She looked like she wished she actually were a real satellite in Earth orbit ...

Anything to be away from these people.

'Yes,' she muttered at last, before pointing and shouting, 'Look, a duck!'

* Hari Socket didn't know it, but he won a fiver at this moment. There'd been a sweepstake running in the town as to when Mrs Wedlock would next speak, instead of uttering her more usual tut. He was the one who had drawn the lucky year.

189

Everyone looked (because ducks are always interesting) but there was no duck, and when they turned back she'd run off. Not at great speed, since she was a woman of late early middle age who was rather fond of cakes. But everyone was too polite to point out that they could still see her pushing through the crowds on the patio, her solar panels flapping and the radar dish on her head spinning slowly. Everybody deserves *some* dignity.*

'Greta,' said Mr Inglebath, 'I'm sorry I ever listened to her. But what can you do?' He shrugged his shoulders as if to say: *Ah! Family!* 'I'll expect the story on my desk first thing Monday morning. OK?'

Greta's heart was beating fast.

She'd got the big story and she'd got her job back. Next stop, the Prilchard-Spritzer Medal, she just knew it. And then, on the first day back at school, she'd stand up in assembly and show them all the medal that *she'd* won in the holidays and that they hadn't, and she'd demand an apology from the Head and that would teach them all a lesson. Ha ha!

* *It was at this point that Sophie Doodad, dressed as a large silvery robot and unbalanced by an accidental nudge from the fleeing woman, fell into the pond with a large silvery splash.*

191

But then she looked down at Jonathon and up at her aunt and a different feeling came over her.

'I can't, Mr Inglebath,' she said sadly. 'There are things about this story that I can't print. People I don't want to embarrass.'

'You mean like DOTTY SCIENTIST BREEDS CAKE THIEF SQUIRREL WITH NUT ALLERGY?' he asked. 'Oh, Tabitha won't mind, will you, Tabs?'

'Well, maybe EMINENT SCIENTIST would read better,' Tabitha suggested, with a smile.

Just then Jessica wobbled over (her Plumulon costume made running awkward) and said, 'Hi, Greta. Look, I won a prize for Best TV-Inspired Alien Costume. I came second.'

'Oh, well done, Jessica,' said Greta. 'What did you win?'

'I won a cake,' said Jessica, holding up a rather large cupcake decorated with a big silver star.

They all had a good laugh at that, even Jessica, who didn't really understand why they were all laughing.*

*She'd watched a lot of TV though and she knew that at the end of a certain sort of show, when the story's over, everyone has a good laugh at something as the picture freezes and the credits start to roll. So she didn't mind not understanding everything.

CHAPTER EIGHTEEN

Deep Space

ROUND ABOUT NOW

THE HUGE SPACE-GOING Robot hurtled through the darkness. It had locked on to a star system just over eight light years away. The journey would take close to 846 years to complete. As it flew it hummed to itself. It had a large store of tunes to hum, twenty or thirty of them, which Harknow-Bumfurly-Histlock had composed himself, 107,242 years earlier. He thought a nice tune might lessen the robot's boredom as it flew for long lifetimes through the emptiness of interstellar space. It didn't lessen the boredom, since he wasn't a very good composer, but the robots had also been programmed to appreciate his effort, so not a single one had ever beamed a complaint back towards Cestrypip.

This was an eleventh generation Huge Space-Going Robot; that is to say, the first Huge Space-Going Robot had left Cestrypip, discovered a planet, destroyed it and built a new, second generation of Huge Space-Going Robots and sent them out into the galaxy. One of those had found a new planet, destroyed it, built a third generation of Huge Space-Going Robots and sent them, in turn, searching for new planets. And so on. This had happened ten times before the

Huge Space-Going Robot had discovered the Earth, and yet its memories of Cestrypip, its dedication to the mission, its desire to please Harknow-Bumfurly-Histlock was exactly the same as if it were the Huge Space-Going Robot the Cestrypian scientist had built himself.

(The maths are simple, if mindboggling: at the present moment there are approximately 360 million Huge Space-Going Robots out there in the galaxy. Approximately sixty million have already beamed reports back to the *Harknow-Bumfurly-Histlock Big Book of Galactic Facts*™; the rest are humming to themselves in deep space, en route to new unexplored stars.)

Unfortunately, twenty years after the launch of the first Huge Space-Going Robots from

Cestrypip, when the robot explorers were merely reaching the first edges of intergalactic space, a series of unfortunate and accidental wildfires swept across Cestrypip's main continent.*

Whole forests of dreaming trees were burnt down (the third stage in the Cestrypian life cycle*), and an entire generation of Cestrypian children grew up without the wisdom of PE teachers. They all became fat, lazy and uncompetitive adults who died of heart disease before having a chance to put down roots. And so, within a few centuries, the entire race vanished from the face of the planet, leaving it silent and empty.

The *Harknow-Bumfurly-Histlock Big Book of Galactic Facts*™ was compiled by giant automated computers buried in the

* Let this be a warning against dropping a smouldering flinfthod in a dry patch of squil. Remember, kids: always take your used flinfthods home with you and dispose of them carefully.

★ See Chapter Two for a reminder.

Croomock mountain range, powered by underground magma fields. Each time a Huge Space-Going Robot beamed a report back to the planet it was added as a new entry. Pictures were annotated, recordings were embedded in the text, facts were collated in charts and graphs.

But no one read it.

For a hundred thousand years the computers have whirred, clicked, buzzed and listened, receiving information and adding to the *Harknow-Bumfurly-Histlock Big Book of Galactic Facts*™ and no one has ever pressed a button beside the screen at the foot of the great Croomock mountain range and scrolled through the entries. No one. Not a single person. Zip. Zero. None.*

However, by the time the Huge Space-Going Robot reached Earth and encountered

* Also, no nuns.

the Great Greta Zargo, another race of intelligent beings, the Lollo-Grags (who had once been pests on the pets the Cestrypippians kept), had been making their homes in the caves of Cestrypip for ten thousand years or more, popping outside each day to tend to their swaying fields of squil. They were a species on their way up, filling the ecological niche left behind by the ancient robot-builders.*

Sometime soon they might discover how to use the keyboard beside the screen at the foot of the Croomock mountain range, and they will see how amazing the universe is, how full of life, and perhaps they will find their way to the entry labelled 'Earth' and might catch an episode of *How Hot Is My Chef?* on the live stream.

Who knows what they will think then?

* This was the first time in their history that they were making use of caves as houses.

POSTLOGUE

Upper Lowerbridge, England, Earth

TWO WEEKS AFTER THE PARTY

I T WAS THE night of the Prilchard-Spritzer Medal Award Ceremony.

Greta Zargo was wearing her smartest trousers.

Jessica Plumb was wearing *her* smartest trousers too.

Aunt Tabitha was with them both and was dressed in her smartest hat.

Wilf Inglebath was with them all and had polished his moustache.

After a short film about the fish pickling and packing process, Mr Prilchard mounted the stage.

'It's my honour,' he said, 'every year to present this here medal to the person what has made the most stunning bit of newspaper writing to my mind in that year what's just gone by. I read them closely. I pay attention. I listen out for the voice what's special, the eye what's keen, the nose what knows a good story.

'I owe a lot to newspapers,' he went on. 'It was in newspapers where the first Christmas offer for Prilchard's Pilchards was printed up. There was a coupon you could cut out and all, and people did, you know, cut them out and brought them in and we sold many, many extra fishes that way. Oh, they were happy times.'

He smiled as he reminisced.

'And so I swore, if ever I had an empire of fishmonger's, I would give something back. And so, here we are, for the fourteenth annual Prilchard-Spritzer Medal Award Ceremony.'

There was a ripple of applause.

'Four stories really caught my eye a lot this year,' he said. 'And they was, in no particular order, number one: SOFA, SO BAD by Fenella Windsock, about the settee what swallowed more than a remote control. Number two: THE BUNS THAT GOT AWAY by Frank Diggory, about the baker's lorry what overturned on the dual carriageway and clogged the East Upperbridge Canal with buns and scones. Number three:

THANK COD IT'S FISHMAS by Dingle D'Lacey, about how a nice bit of fish can be a cost-effective replacement for turkey or goose at the Christmas table. And number four: UPPER LOWERBRIDGE MYSTERY CAKE THIEF APPREHENDED AT SPACE PARTY BY INTREPID REPORTER by Greta Zargo, in which a squirrel was caught nicking some cakes.'

The announcement of each newspaper headline brought a little ripple of applause from the four tables scattered around the back room of Prilchard's big shop in Upper Lowerbridge's high street.

'And the winner is …' Mr Prilchard announced, ripping open a golden envelope. He left a long pause after the word 'is', like they always do on *Dance, Baker, Dance!* There was an imaginary drum roll in the air.

'Dingle D'Lacey for THANK COD IT'S FISHMAS. Well done, Dingle.'

Greta clapped politely, even though her shoulders slumped.

If only, she thought to herself, she'd found a bigger story, a better story, something more important than a series of stolen cakes. Maybe a squirrel with a sweet tooth simply wasn't enough. After all, she had to admit, it was hardly the end of the world, was it? But she could only write the stories that came her way, only write the ones that landed on her doorstep. She could only pick up the ends of threads she found and follow them, and if Mr Prilchard didn't think they were interesting enough for a medal, then so be it. She realised in that moment that maybe this job wasn't about medals and awards and showing off at school. Maybe it really was all about serving her duty to The Truth.

'I don't like fish,' said Jessica. 'It makes me burp fishy burps. I'd rather get a box of biscuits for Christmas than a trout.'

'Do you know,' Mr Inglebath whispered, leaning towards them as Dingle D'Lacey began his short speech of *thank you*s and *I told you so*s, 'that's the fourteenth year in a row a story encouraging people to buy more fish has won the Prilchard-Spritzer Medal?'

'Oh,' whispered Greta, sitting up straight. 'I'm beginning to see a pattern, Mr Inglebath. I think there might be something *fishy* going on.'

They all laughed at that, even Jessica.

Fortunately Dingle D'Lacey had just made a joke in his acceptance speech, so it didn't seem like they were being rude.

'No, but seriously,' Greta whispered, when the chuckling had died down, 'I think I might have an idea for a new story, Mr Inglebath. An exposé on corruption in the world of journalistic prizes and fishmongery.'*

'That's my girl,' said Mr Inglebath.

'I've invented a telepathic pencil,' her aunt said. 'You hold it in your hand and it writes whatever you're thinking. I thought it might come in handy.'

'That's brilliant,' Greta said, giving her aunt a hug. 'Thanks for believing in me.'

The four of them skipped the Prilchard-Spritzer Medal buffet, it being comprised mostly of fishcakes, and they all having had quite enough to do with cakes for the time being.

They walked out into the cool of the summer evening.

* She had just remembered Clause Forty-Two (B) from her parents' Last Will and Testament: Greta, darling, always think three times before trusting a fishmonger with your dry-cleaning.

Above them a thousand stars twinkled and glittered in the deep blue sky.

Greta wondered if there was anyone out there, on a planet circling one of those stars, looking back at her. It was one of the Big Questions, wasn't it? And one that she'd probably never know the answer to.

She did know, however, that there was a new tin of hot chocolate powder waiting for her when she got home, and a fresh packet of cheese that she could slice and put on top of some nice hot toast.

She hadn't won the prize, but still, it wasn't such a bad life being Greta Zargo.

COULD YOU BE A REPORTER LIKE GRETA?

WERE YOU PAYING ATTENTION?

TAKE THIS QUIZ AND FIND OUT!

1. Whose cake went missing first?
- *a)* Hari Socket
- *b)* Harknow-Bumfurly-Histlock
- *c)* Agnes Nottin-Thisbok

2. What kind of cake was stolen from Mrs Hummock?
- *a)* A fishcake
- *b)* A bicycle
- *c)* A sponge with peanut butter fondant icing

3. Who was the Swiss roll stolen from?
- *a)* Oscar Teachbaddly
- *b)* King Magnus III, Lord of Wind
- *c)* Harrerf

4. How old was Greta when she solved her first case (The Riddle of the Missing Asparagus)?
- *a)* 96
- *b)* A bicycle
- *c)* 4

5. Where was Oscar Teachbaddly's cake before it was stolen?
- *a)* In his stomach
- *b)* On the arm of his armchair
- *c)* On a pirate ship, sailing the six seas

6. What important clue did Greta find in her kitchen?

a) A bicycle
b) A few tufty grey hairs
c) King Magnus III, Lord of Bins

7. Who was Greta's prime suspect?

a) Bertie Rustle
b) President Slightly
c) Agnes Nottin-Thisbok

8. Who was the cake thief?

a) Jonathan
b) King Magnus III, Lord of Fibs
c) Greta Zargo

9. What is Jonathan allergic to?

a) peas
b) peas and nuts
c) peanuts

10. What really happened to Mrs Hummock's cake?

a) A bicycle
b) She ate it
c) Nothing. Nothing at all

**LOOK OUT FOR GRETA'S
NEXT ADVENTURE IN:**

GRETA ZARGO

AND THE
AMOEBA MONSTERS
FROM THE MIDDLE OF THE EARTH

COMING SOON!

Turn over for a sneak peek and see what
Greta gets up to next …

PROLOGUE

Untold Miles Beneath the Earth's Crust

FIVE MONTHS AGO (WEDNESDAY)

SOMETHING HAD WOKEN. Something ancient. Something unnamed. Something that should not have been woken.

Deep in the Earth. Beneath the deepest well, below the deepest mine, further down than the deepest potholer's pothole. It was deep down there, down where the sleepers had slept for untold ages. Dark. Hot. Silent.

And then ... *scrunch, scrunch, scrunch* ... the shovel came digging. A simple electric shovel that had been invented by a kindly aunt to help one little girl with her gardening, and now ... it had dug too deep.

Things that had dwelt in darkness, chewing slowly on sad rocks, had their world cracked open, like an egg hatching. And so they began to climb, inching slowly up the shaft, squeezing stickily between sheer, muddy rock walls.

Above them a new world waited.

They knew nothing of sunlight, but soon it would touch them.

They knew nothing of fresh air, but soon it would surround them.

They knew nothing of people, but soon they would eat them.

And so, they climbed, and above them

the world slept, unaware of the horror that approached, unaware of the threat rising from the depths, unaware that the final end had begun.

Now read on ...

CHAPTER ONE

Greta Zargo's House, Upper Lowerbridge, England, Earth

LAST SATURDAY (BREAKFAST-TIME)

WHEN GRETA ZARGO'S parents accidentally died she was left the family home, everything in it, a large bank account, two black and white posters of kittens falling over, a lifetime subscription to *Paperclip World* (*the* magazine for all paperclip enthusiasts) and a pair of trousers she'd one day grow into. Since she had only been a baby at the time, all of this was held in trust by her Aunt Tabitha until Greta's eighth birthday.[*]

As soon as she turned eight Greta moved out of her aunt's house and into her own one, just over the road. Naturally her aunt kept an eye on Greta, as often as she could, and in the three years that followed absolutely no disasters had occurred. Other than perhaps that one time when the emus stole Mr Borris's wig and he wrote an outraged letter to the President about it. But even then, as Greta pointed out in a stiffly worded article in the school newspaper, it *was* a very funny-looking wig, and the President had never actually replied to Mr Borris anyway.[★] So, no disasters at all. None.

* *This rather early age for independence was due to a legally binding spelling mistake ('eighth' where it should have said 'eighteenth') in her parents' Last Will and Testament.*

★ *Although the President of Britain, Aethelred Slightly, had been at school with Mr Borris many years before, Mr Borris tended to overestimate how memorable and, indeed, how likeable he'd been as a child.*

This morning Greta was up early. It was the first day of the autumn school holiday and she was grumpy. Grumpy because the sun had barely made an effort outside the window to warm the world. Grumpy because the only clean socks she had were yesterday's dirty ones. And grumpy because of the general awful earliness of the getting up.

Greta believed that the holidays were not the time for early rising. Although, to be fair, she didn't think school days were days for early rising either. The Head, however, had sent her home with enough letters to give to herself, asking her to make sure that she was at school on time, and that several times a week she arrived at school almost in time to not quite be told off. For other children the Head would have sent letters home addressed to their parents, but, for electric current through a pile of Norwegian goatherds who'd just been passing round a helium balloon.

But the singing wasn't even the worst thing about the cat. At least you *knew* that once the sun had gone down the yodel would soon be coming. It wasn't a surprise, and it was the cat's surprises that Greta hated most.

It had a habit of sneaking into her house and hiding dead mice in her knicker drawer.

When she wasn't expecting it.

That was the thing she hated most.

But, as a proverb her aunt had invented said: *Cats do as cats do and there's nothing to do about cats doing what they do, so you'd best accept it and move on and try not to make eye contact and, to be honest, I prefer squirrels, Greta — much friendlier on the whole and also furry.* It wasn't a great proverb, and her aunt had got distracted halfway through making it, but luckily inventing proverbs was only a very small part of what Aunt Tabitha did, and most of the other parts tended to go much better.

Greta gave the cat a grumpy glower and pedalled off in the direction of elsewhere without once looking back.

As she cycled her grumpiness began to clear away.

* * *

Greta worked, in her spare time, as an unpaid volunteer junior reporter for *The Local Newspaper*,* reporting personally to Wilf Inglebath, the editor. She was always looking for a Big Story that would make the front page, her name and people gasp. And today she thought she might have one.

* An award-winning newspaper, as it boasted on the front cover. It had won the Most Expensive Free Newspaper prize three years running, until one of the judges realised there was something wrong with their prize, and it wasn't awarded last year.

She pedalled through the quiet streets of Upper Lowerbridge and out of town, towards the Hester Sometimes Conference Centre and Immobile Library. It was in the conference centre that Greta was due to meet her aunt, who was hosting and organising the Twelfth Annual Festival of New Stuff (TAFoNS, for short).

If a whole bunch of scientists presenting the New Stuff they had made and discovered, in a converted stately home just outside Upper Lowerbridge, wasn't the sort of thing that would make a great story for *The Local Newspaper*, then Greta was a haddock. Which she wasn't. *

As she turned the last corner and free-wheeled down the long, straight drive towards the Hester Sometimes Conference Centre and Immobile Library, the sun came

* She even had the paperwork to prove it, were such a thing necessary.

out and the last tendrils of fog disappeared into wherever it was that fog went. *

Weeeee, thought Greta as the wind whippled her hair.

She skidded to a halt in front of the entrance and read half of the sign that was stuck to the automatic sliding glass doors.

She stood very still and waited for the doors to forget she was there and close themselves again, and then she read the rest of the sign.

The sign said: Twelfth Annual Festival of New Stuff (TAFoNS, for short) is Cancelled.

Oh, she thought.

Three further thoughts followed close on the heels of the Oh.

Firstly: *I didn't need to get up so early, after all.*

* No one knew for sure where this was. The only expedition, led in 1978 by the great poet Albert Rhymeswell, never returned from wherever it was they went

228

Secondly: *Well, that's my Big Story up the spout.*

And thirdly: *I'd best go find Aunt Tabitha and see what's what.*

CHAPTER TWO

Greta Zargo's Back Garden, Upper Lowerbridge, England, Earth

LAST SATURDAY (JUST AFTER BREAKFAST)

SLOWLY THE GELATINOUS blob slumphed its way over the edge of the hole. Bits of mud and flecks of grit writhed on its surface, like currants swirling on top of a giant, transparent, jelly-ish cake.

The cat that Greta had glowered grumpily

at a few minutes earlier was called Major Influence and he ate one in every four birds that landed in Greta's garden, even though it wasn't his garden. It only took him a moment to notice the wriggling, squirming shape that had emerged from the great hole and wonder whether it was something he could eat.

He sniffed it.

As he sniffed the gooey blob tapped him on the nose with a small, gooey, blobby protrusion.

It was how a gelatinous thing sniffed back.

Major Influence jumped at the cold, oozy, strange touch, but found that his jump didn't take him nearly as far as his jump normally took him.

In fact, it hadn't taken him anywhere.

The thing was still touching his nose. It was stuck there.

He flipped over and began kicking at the jelly-like blob with his back legs, hissing and clawing like a furious furry miniature lawnmower. But ... it was no good.

Slowly, hair by hair, whisker by whisker, ear by ear, the oozing jelly blob surrounded the struggling cat until the poor thing was entirely inside it, floating helplessly.

And then the thing paused. It sat there, pulsating and throbbing and writhing, and it began to digest its first ever above-ground meal.

On the fence three sparrows and a blackbird watched with interest. They approved of the removal of Major Influence and they would have applauded if they had hands. But they didn't. So they didn't.

From out of the great dark hole at the bottom of Greta's garden a second, slightly larger, slightly blobbier wobbling form began to emerge. It hauled itself over the muddy lip, out on to the dewy lawn, with a deep, slow slurphing-slumping sound.

About the Author and Illustrator

A.F. HARROLD is an English poet who writes and performs for adults and children. He spends his time showing off on stage, writing poems and books, and stroking his beard (it helps churn the ideas). He lives in Reading with a stand-up comedian and two cats. His favourite cake is Battenberg.

JOE TODD-STANTON lives in Bristol and likes to skate and play table tennis in his spare time. As a child he was addicted to comics and the Cartoon Network. If he could be any book character, he would be Winnie the Pooh as he seems to have it all figured out. Pooh's very humble and never takes life too seriously. Joe's favourite cake is cheesecake.

HAVE YOU READ ALL OF FIZZLEBERT STUMP'S ADVENTURES?

Fizzlebert Stump lives in a travelling circus. He hangs around with acrobats, plays the fool with clowns, and puts his head in a lion's mouth every night. But it can be a bit lonely being the only kid in the circus. So one day, Fizz decides to join a library – and that's when it all goes terribly wrong …

The bearded Barboozul family are the new stars of Fizzlebert Stump's circus. Their act is full of magic, mystery, fun and fear. But then things start to go wrong. The lion loses his dentures. The clowns lose their noses. The Ringmaster loses his temper. And the circus is about to lose its licence. Is the bearded boy to blame?

When Fish the sea lion goes missing, Fizzlebert tracks down the runaway beast to the Aquarium, with its piratical owner Admiral Spratt-Haddock. But the Aquarium has problems of its own. Fish (not Fish the sea lion, *fish*. Keep up) are going missing, and the Admiral blames the circus. Can Fizzlebert solve the mystery?

HAVE YOU READ FIZZLEBERT'S FOURTH ADVENTURE?

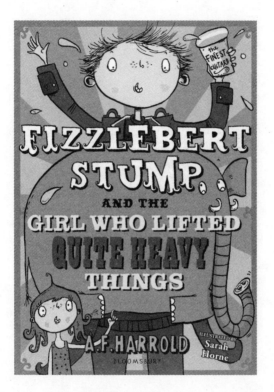

It's the great Circus of Circuses competition, and Fizzlebert Stump has no act. He's no longer the Boy Who Puts His Head in the Lion's Mouth – the lion retired. Can Fizz find a new act in time? Can the Bearded Boy find his long-lost parents? And can their new friend Alice, secret Strongwoman, find her rightful place in the circus?

HAVE YOU READ FIZZLEBERT'S FIFTH ADVENTURE

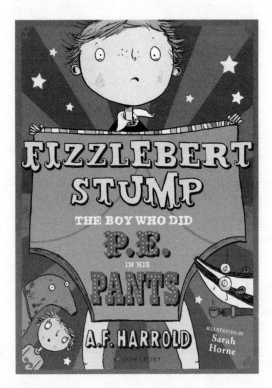

After being lost in the woods and mistaken for a very rude girl, Fizzlebert Stump suddenly finds himself at school. It's certainly different to his usual life of training to be a strongman and playing football with a sea lion! But why won't anyone believe Fizz belongs in the circus? Will he ever make it back? Or will he have to sit up straight and pay attention forever?

Disaster has struck! The Ringmaster has sold the circus, and the new owner is forcing everyone to work at his supermarket. But Fizz and his friends are no good at stacking shelves or selling spuds, and, worst of all, their uniforms feature no sequins whatsoever ... Can Fizz find a way to save the circus? Or will they have to put up with Mr Pinkbottle and his annoying clipboard forever?